GODFREE
BEELZEBUB'S
MASQUERADE

GODFREE
BEELZEBUB'S
MASQUERADE

JOHN F. MORKEN

Author Photo captured by Dina Morrison
Cover design by John F. Morken

ISBN: 978-1-63901-478-1 (Paperback Edition)
ISBN: 978-1-63901-479-8 (Hardcover Edition)
ISBN: 978-1-63901-476-7 (E-book Edition)

Some characters and events in this book are fictitious. Any similarity to the real persons, living or dead, is coincidental and not intended by the author.

Book Ordering Information

Phone Number: 315 288-7939 ext. 1000 or 347-901-4920
Email: info@globalsummithouse.com
Global Summit House
www.globalsummithouse.com

www.johnmorken.com

Printed in the United States of America

Also by

JOHN F. MORKEN

· · · · · · · · · ·

The Green Teas Cave

The Golden Hinde Conspiracy

FOR MY FATHER

1. **Evil**: the same old thing.

No matter what happens, keep this in mind: It's the same old thing, from one end of the world to the other. It fills the history books, ancient and modern, and the cities, and the houses too. Nothing new at all.

Familiar, transient. – **Marcus Aurelius (Book Seven)**

2. Profoundly immoral and wicked.

Please allow me to introduce myself

I'm a man of wealth and taste

I've been around for a long, long year

Stole many a man's soul and faith.

Sympathy for the Devil – **The Rolling Stones**

. . . .

Him the Almighty Power

Hurled headlong flaming from the ethereal sky.

With hideous ruin and combustion, down

To bottomless perdition, there to dwell,

In adamantine chains and penal fire,

Who durst defy the Omnipotent to arms.

– Paradise Lost by John Milton – Book 1

. . . .

And no Wonder, for even Satan disguises
himself as an angel of light.

2 Corinthians 11:14

PREAMBLE

For a fallen Angel, finding redemption for my many offenses against God is difficult. Discarded by The Almighty, I started a new job here on Earth. That was 2,000 years ago. Officially, I now serve Lucifer. My name is Beelzebub, founder and current headmaster of the Order of the Fly.

My offense, you ask? I killed my older brother, Dagon, with an archangel blade - the only weapon capable of killing my kind.

Currently, the World is overheating and becoming a dirty, unkempt place. Arguably, humans are incapable of learning from history – the facts that occurred before you were born. Sadly, you have no idea what's coming, given your ignorance of the past and failure to learn from history. News flash: it does repeat itself.

Marcus Aurelius was right: Nothing new at all.

Over the years, I've touched so many souls - some more evil than the rest. I have my favorites, of course. The worst of the worst left an indelible and bloody stain on the Earth. Some of their evil deeds were, in large part, accomplished with my duplicitous help. And still others, you created on your own, without my influence or *touch*.

For sure, some humans fall prey to bad luck and become victims of unfortunate circumstances. Whether you're in the wrong place at the right time or just plain stupid, lousy luck eventually catches up with all of us at some point in time. In the long run, the law of averages will place misfortune at your doorstep and cause inevitable pain and suffering, just like it did to me.

But not all humans are bad or evil, just like not all angels are good or bad. Like myself, some fall into the middle and play with the human condition as a form of entertainment. It's just good fun to break the law of averages on occasion – trust me. It's just good fun to move molecules and *touch* people.

I've also seen many natural disasters during my time here on Earth. Whether it be flood, famine, or fire, they always end the same way with widespread and profound suffering. You might say natural disasters are a necessary but unfortunate part of the human experience.

Then there is this: sometimes several unrelated, different people, their ideas, and unexpected tragic events merge into one, causing a calamity of sorts. It can happen anywhere - a perfect human storm, better known as a catastrophe.

Because it is the human condition, in my opinion, to suffer disappointment and grave hardship, such tragedies or catastrophes have become relatively commonplace.

Ultimately, and in the end, human tragedies are your story - The Human Story.

CHAPTER ONE

66666666666666666666666666666666666

Falling From Heaven – 30 CE

To Earth, my Father sent me as punishment for killing my older brother, Dagon. He had it coming. As a result, however, my father expelled me from Heaven indefinitely. I am now a fallen angel and Prince of all lower Demons.

You should know, upon arrival I met a man named John, whom you call an Apostle or the Baptist. He was my one true friend and the younger brother of James. The oldest brother of the two, Andrew, was an odd man with known proclivities for deviant sex. Andrew also cared for the ill and deformed – a doctor of sorts. He was an excellent doctor. Unfortunately, Andrew became a pariah, probably due to his greed, lust, and avarice, which made him susceptible to my touch.

On the other hand, John the Baptist teased me, given his loyalty to his brothers and fellow Christians. As I said, John was my friend, or I initially believed him to be someone I could influence, persuade, and touch. Unfortunately, John betrayed me with devotion and love for humanity. He was a member of a relatively obscure religious sect that called themselves Christians. They believed Jesus of Nazareth was the incarnation or Son of my father, God. Eventually, John and his fellow Christians turned on me, casting me out for not being capable of human love.

"Human love?" I asked myself. "What is it?"

Being incapable of understanding what human love is, I plotted a course filled with as much deception and trickery as possible. I mostly sought revenge, however. My father, your God, expelled me from Heaven and, as a result, my remaining brothers laughed at my misfortune. I was humiliated and bitter. Their chicanery pushed me towards affection for the worst that men can do.

I would lie about the truth for my single purpose of causing a riot or overthrowing a government. For me, I just wanted to wreak havoc on society. As it turned out, lies, repeated over time and often enough, have dire consequences. They can stir up a revolt and cause violent insurrections, and there is nothing more entertaining than a violent insurrection.

I became fierce and cruel, seeking to devour all of humanity through deceit and dishonesty. I was proud of my corruption and preyed upon anyone susceptible to my duplicitous, unscrupulous double-dealings. I did not care for humans anymore; for one of them, the nicest, betrayed me, and I didn't know why. From now on, at least until my father forgave me, I would be evil - a son of God committed to evil. I sought out mostly men with defective souls and angry hearts. It wasn't that difficult.

"Come closer, my child, let me see you," I said to him.

He was the son of Caligula, but most folks don't know that to be true. Trust me, my children, as sanguinity goes, this kid was born in 37 CE from Caligula. I watched it, pulled from his mother's birth canal and given the name Lucius Domitius Ahenobarbus. Many years later, he started to blossom into my instrument of evil. I called him Nero.

"Who are you?" young Nero asked me, scared from the fall he had just endured.

"A friend," I said with my crooked fingers crossed. "But you can call me Annaeus Seneca or teacher," I told the young Caesar. Of course, we fallen angels tend to lie and take on many human forms.

Young Nero was eleven years of age when I reintroduced myself. He grew up in the port town of Antium, thirty or so miles southwest of Rome. He wasn't a bad kid, just impressionable and susceptible to evil.

"You are my teacher?" he asked.

"I am your tutor, and you have been assigned to me," I said to him. "When you need advice, I'll lend it, my child," I explained. "For now, let's practice your singing," I instructed.

Being an angel, I gave him a divine voice and a well-trained elocutionist, but that did very little to quell or soften his lust for evil duty. Some years later, in July, Nero fell prey to the killing bug and, because of it, nearly brought the Roman Empire to ruin. Those were good times. Up until then, Nero was content to poison his enemies, including his stepbrother, Britannicus. That was probably my fault.

"I don't have to listen to Agrippina anymore; I am the Emperor and do as I please," he complained to me about his mother. In response, I suggested that he get rid of her so that we could do whatever we want. He took to it so well, losing all sense of right and wrong. Nero was a natural born killer.

Nero also inherited his father's perverse sexual appetite and propensity toward violence. Before long, he started sleeping with many of the senators' wives and daughters. Given my influence, Nero kept young boys chained to his bed and would rape them regularly. He had no preference between men or women and, on occasion would even tie down a pig and rape his dinner before slicing the beast's throat open. When his mother protested his actions, he had his lover, Pythagoras, execute and feed her to the lions. For Pythagoras' efforts, Nero married him and showered him with vast riches.

"What shall we do today?" Nero asked Pythagoras without a sign of remorse.

Of course, I always touched Pythagoras before he would answer Nero.

"Let's kill some Christians," he responded.

I always enjoyed killing Christians. John made sure of that. We would ride in the chariot that Augustus charted for his triumphs back in the day when Caesar traveled to Rome. Along the way, Nero and his boy lover, Pythagoras, would frequently stop, beheading and crucifying as many Christians that they could lay their drunken hands on. During this madness, they tortured and killed the disciple Peter. When that got tiresome, they raped women and torched entire villages while watching the Catholics get impaled and burned alive.

"What's for lunch?" Nero asked after the morning's rampage.

Once in Rome, before arriving at his *Golden House*, Nero liked to enter through the Circus Maximus arch. After, we would make our way across the Velabrum and the Forum to the Palatine and Apollo Temple. Along the way, Nero would stop to speak to the unsuspecting citizens of Rome, only to order them burned on a freshly planted stake or just disemboweled for a perceived insult. He also called for many Christians to be eviscerated and hanged for his diabolical pleasure. Nero was honestly mad in his effort to kill them.

Given his rage, as a young Caesar, Nero kept a large platoon of praetorian cohorts, military ensigns, and standards. With all those men at his side, Nero ordered them to perform unspeakable acts of violence. Given his well-protected and unstoppable wantonness, cruelty, extravagance, lust, avarice, and perversion,

I never really offered my assistance; the boy was a natural, dispensing his vicious cruelty at will and without repercussion.

· · · · · · · · · ·

At night, we would hit the town.

"Slave, fetch me my purple robe and the Greek cloak adorned with stars of gold," he would demand. "And round up five or six harlots and dancing girls for dinner."

His dominance was impressive.

We would eat all types of food prepared by Rome's finest Chefs. If the food was deemed inedible, Nero would boil the Chef to death. As a result, we very rarely tasted a lousy meal. After most of those perfect meals, Nero would sing a few songs, but never without his elocutionist by his side, always ready to warn him to spare his voice.

One evening, he developed a sore throat, probably due to the massive amounts of grain alcohol and decent wine he loved to consume. Nero was a drunk, and so were his many sycophants, which made his actions so shocking to the sober fool. Sober fools didn't last long in Nero's circle. They didn't get it. As an angel, when fools start believing, my fun and games can begin. Nevertheless, because of his brainwash, Nero blamed the elocutionist for his sore throat, threw him into a pit of deadly vipers, then vomited the entire contents of his belly all over the dying musician. It was somewhat difficult to stomach and possibly the most distasteful act of violence I have ever witnessed. But then, things changed.

"Time for some pranks," Nero suggested after that act. "Come, teacher, join me for a riotous walk home," he stated with some red and yellow bile dripping from his mouth.

"Of course, dear boy," I happily replied.

On such occasions, he disguised himself and rambled through Rome's taverns and crowded streets - beating, stabbing, and robbing men on their way home. As I watched, Nero broke into shops and stole honest men's wares. After his rampage, his folly's proceeds were spent on his debaucherous floats down the river Tiber to Ostia on the Tyrrhenian Sea.

On Sundays, during July, we would float down the river Tiber to his palace in Ostia. Back then, tents were set up at various intervals along the banks and fitted with slave women and boys. Nero would violate every woman's orifice at each stop, then remove their reproductive organs and toss them into the river like gutted trout. Unfortunately, the helpless boys were castrated, then raped and beheaded. On those bloody Sundays, I kept my distance from Nero, always taking the lead boat to watch the river turn red on my stops.

"Bring me Sporus, I want to make a woman out of him," he screamed with bloodshot eyes. "After, we shall marry, so bring him with us," Nero demanded.

Sporus was one of the lucky ones. Nero married the boy in a grand ceremony at his house in Ostia and spent a fortune on his guests. He kept many castrated freedmen as wives and, for the most part, treated them fairly, only if they imitated the cries of a deflowered virgin by his relatively tiny uncut cock.

At his marriage ceremony, Nero covered himself with the skin of a male lion, let himself loose from a golden cage, and devoured, with his teeth, the sexual organs and other private parts of men and women who he had bound to stakes. The staking was particularly gruesome and took place before dinner – in front of the slaves. For them, it was a lottery of sorts.

Nevertheless, Nero loved to entertain his guests. He even bit off a slave's penis and forced it down a bound woman's throat until she choked to death. Imagine shoving a disemboweled and castrated man's penis down a woman's throat until she suffocated to death as a form of entertainment.

"Are you not entertained!" he shouted to his intoxicated guests wholly covered in the blood, shit, and warm urine of his slave victims.

"Time for a song... and to attend to my prey!" he finished. Which meant he wanted his physicians to cut the veins of the staked men and women who had not died from their wounds or his bites. All of them were ravaged and died soon after that. Given the Roman culture at that time, the members of his wedding party barely noticed the gore. If they did, then it was no different than watching a boy fillet a fish on the Ostia riverbank.

Dinner, which was unnecessary for me, was truthfully bothersome. For me, watching the boys shake uncontrollably before being raped or castrated or beheaded soured the evening.

I never felt the need to kill women because they were always sacred, according to God, and frightened souls were immune to my deception, which made them boring. Of course, Nero enjoyed the look of unmasked horror on his fellow human beings and loved to kill them all. It was then, during the public slaughter of his people, and his treatment of women, that I took my leave from Nero.

· · · · · · · · · ·

Women are sacred, according to everything I know to be true. They are makers of life, genetically built to protect and save humanity. My dad taught me that. So, after Nero's violence against women, my interest in him began to fade. It began on the eighteenth day of July during the year 64 CE.

Nero had grown tired and bored with his routines of murder, crucifixion, burning, and starving Christians to death. I suppose, letting loose a pack of ravenous wild dogs to tear Christians apart made him feel healthy, powerful, and whole. I don't know. At that point, when everyone was dying, I didn't care. But, after looking into his eyes, I discovered a new vicious animal inside, and it wasn't my doing. Nero was genuinely evil, capable of the worst crimes that human beings could inflict upon each other. He was never affected and always ready to inflict more diabolical pain and suffering upon his fellow mankind.

"This old city is disgusting," he complained. "My Golden House needs a new wing."

"But the night is windy, Nero," I said, dwelling on my love of fire.

"Then maybe we should just find some whores or pigs to gut?" he suggested.

"No," I replied, feeling, in a sense, some form of concern for women.

"Look at all the narrow streets and wooden homes, Caesar. Wouldn't you prefer to see a city made of marble and stone in the Greek style, with wide streets and pedestrian arcades and fewer Christians?" I suggested.

"I do hate Christians," he responded. "What do you have in mind?"

"Well, the merchant area of the City has grown vile, and there is talk of malaria spreading. Send some of your standards with torches and let's cleanse the marketplace of disease and Christians," I offered.

"Perfect!" he shouted with a roar after accidentally shitting in his robe once again. "Oops, you there, come clean me, I'm dirty," he instructed a slave as he dropped his robe. "We shall blame the Christians and build my new golden home after they are dead and burned to dust."

"Grab that boy, the blue-eyed one, he will be a useful torch after I fuck him," Nero yelled while looking down on the many shops filled with flammable goods. The Circus Maximus was only a stone's throw away.

"Why the boy, what about your new husband, Sporus?" I asked him.

"Because I want him to burn, teacher, the insignificant little shit needs to burn," he replied.

Nero then vomited out most of his guts, then crapped himself again, laughing in between each wretched chunder and shit.

"Besides, he's Carthaginian, isn't he?" was Nero's rationale as he coughed up green snot and shot nasty vomit from his red nose. I watched in disgust, as the vile blood red and yellow shit ran down his backside, soiling his arrogant purple wardrobe.

"Yes, I guess he is," I answered in disbelief.

Ultimately, violence and gore became too addictive to young Nero, making him ignorant and numb to his surrounding environment.

CHAPTER TWO

666666666666666666666666666666666666

THE EVIL MEN DO

I suppose Rome had it coming. Nothing like an excellent conflagration to sanitize a dirty and vile city. Without much hesitation, I touched Nero one last time. The result would be devastatingly extravagant.

"I will torch the City," Nero screamed at me while raping the unfortunate Carthaginian boy to death. I never did get his name.

"Tell me, given everything we have accomplished, why tonight?" he asked me.

"Because we can, dear Caesar, because we can," I explained to the bloodthirsty man.

Nero unleashed himself from the dead boy, then grabbed his flute and began to dance and play. After a short while, he tossed the flute off the balcony of his palace, picked up his violin, and began singing the "Sack of Ilium" in perfect harmony with his notes and chords.

"Throw the torch where the goods are stored. We will blame it on the Christians," he shouted. "Come, teacher, we shall watch from the Tower of Maecenas on the Esquiline Hill."

The fire started small, near the Circus Maximus, where lions ripped slaves apart. It rapidly expanded along the Palatine and Caelian slopes. With the help of a robust, warm wind, nearly every district of Rome became engulfed in flames. The Temple of Jupiter Stator, Domus Transitora, the Circus Maximus,

House of the Vestals, and the Forum were all consumed then destroyed by fire. People were burned alive.

"Ha, look at them burn," he said. "Don't you love a good Christian bonfire?" Nero asked me.

"Yes, my son, of course," I replied.

The progress of the flames quickly destroyed my pupil's home - Nero's Palace.

"Let them all burn while I play my song," he said, jumping up and down and slapping his own ass.

"And then what, the City of Rome is burning to the ground!" I pointed out to him.

The fire spread fast, forcing us to flee the city. Along the way, about four miles outside the city, we encountered the legions of Germany and gangs of Christians who had declared Nero a public enemy of the people. Without his disguise, the mob soon began to shout and encircle Nero. It only took one precisely thrown stone to draw first blood, striking Nero on his forehead and setting off the hungry hordes of German legions, freedmen, and vengeful Christians.

I noticed his cock, totally taken away by the sword of a German soldier. Another Christian man from the Emerald Island swung a left hook, knocking his nose flat.

Badly broken, Nero was eventually throated with a dagger by an imposing Spanish freedman.

When his soul was leaving his body, a large male lion fleeing from the confines of the burning Circus Maximus, locked onto his neck and crushed the life out of him. His weight and strength were mighty. Imagine a large African male lion, finally free, with the taste for humans in his mouth, setting upon Nero. It was gruesomely awesome.

While happily eating Nero, the large male cat eventually shared him with two more junior hungry lionesses, and together, they aggressively tore Nero's torso apart. Watching the lions devour his bloody body, including his cock and balls, gave me some unanticipated relief. As I watched the lions rip him into pieces, it made me feel good. After the lions ate his brains, liver, and heart, I reckoned, it was time to go.

All told, it was disgusting to watch and even worse to remember. The large cats were bigger and better than the Germans and the Christians but they left them alone. Ultimately, given their nature, the cats ran off into the night, keeping Nero's body parts for their offspring.

Days After, the lionesses took down what they needed, primarily for their king's hunger. The lion king, Kodjo, demanded that his queens kill every sheep, deer, pig, cow, and occasional peasant they could put their claws on.

"When they run," Kodjo would say, "then have some fun, and if they whine, then throttle their throats."

Kodjo was a tyrant and loved to kill. Over time, the pride of lions grew to twenty or so, with Kodjo always in charge.

"Feed me, my lovelies, for I am your king," he would say while slopping over a dead animal or human. This overkill might have continued but for the actions of Kodjo's defective son.

"Where is Unika? The little brat needs some discipline," he would roar. The many scars the king left on Unika's face gave the boy more than enough reason to disobey and hate his father. He often acted out by hunting and killing humans. Although Kodjo did his best to discipline his delinquent son, he was ultimately too bloodthirsty for power and sex.

"Stop boy, you must not anger our father with your needless kills and avarice," Kudjo demanded. "We are only allowed to kill what we need to survive, and we don't need the Grizzlies coming down upon us, do we?" the lion king warned. However, because of the hatred he felt toward his father, Unika kept killing humans. His juvenile actions eventually angered God, so he ordered the bears to make short work of Kudjo and his entire pride of lions for the insult.

God blessed the Grizzly Bear. We learned that in school. When it became known to the dominant Grizzly, Arktos, that the cats were parading into his territory and violating my father's rules, he became angry. Without haste, Arktos sent every male and female grizzly bear south into the Italian Alps and beyond to hunt and kill his natural-born enemies. Especially the juvenile delinquent, Unika.

"Kill every one of them, and bring me that bastard son Unika's head," Arktos demanded.

"Take bub with you; to account for your actions, of course," he said to the bear army captain.

"I'm better off with you, Arktos; I'm heading north, after all," I begged.

"NOO," he growled.

Arktos was 12 feet tall, weighed 2000 pounds, and made horses' whimper.

"Beez, I know you are unhappy and have done bad things, but your father is my friend, and after what happened with the cats and your plaything, Nero, you must atone for this," Arktos said.

"But Nero is dead, Arktos, and I do not like the cats. Please, let me go forth," I begged.

"Forth?" Arktos roared. "Dear boy, there is an army of cats down south…and they think it's ok to eat humans. What shall I tell your father when he finds out you did not help us?" he shouted.

"Tell him the winter came, and you were hibernating; it's almost time, isn't it?"

"Not for the cats, Beez. Time is not on their side, dear boy. We must kill the cats," Arktos instructed. "Your father's orders are final."

"They're just cats, Your Majesty. Send twenty of your best and be done with it," I suggested.

"HMMM," the great bear king grumbled in reply.

"Send him to Septimus, husband. I will not have a coward amongst our ranks!" the queen then said.

Wilhelmina was the bear queen and nearly as big as Arktos.

"We don't need him," she continued. "Besides, I hear he is afraid of horses." That gathered many stupid bear laughs.

Next to horses, bears are my father's favorite creation. They are at the top of the food chain by design and loyal to a fault. Even the big cats were no match for the grizzly bears, especially when my father ordered them to end their reign of terror. The silent but strong types always worried me. Before long, and in short order, the bears started killing and eating every big cat in the region. The bear captain eventually brought Unika's head to Arktos, which he promptly gave to his youngest son to eat. Kudjo fled to Spain, where he was ultimately caught and killed by some humans. He now sits stuffed and mounted on the wall of some Persian general's palace.

After ending Kudjo's reign of terror, the grizzly bears headed north to hibernate, and I tagged along, free of Nero and all the blood-soaked violence. For me, it was time to breathe some fresh air.

CHAPTER THREE

VILLA DE PRIMUS SEPTIMUS – 69 CE

For you people, the Common Era was an opportunity to grow the vegetables and raise the beasts, as my father intended. He completely underestimated your love of war. As it turns out, the large-scale killing of your own kind has remained a uniquely human trait. You idiots made that one up all by yourselves. Romans, in particular, had a love affair with war. But so did the Huns, Mongols, Visigoths and my least favorite of all – the Vandals.

After Nero died and the lion campaign ended in victory, I kept walking north through Tuscany, Bologna, Ferrara, and Venice. I can't say what drove me north. Maybe I needed a vacation.

"Never too much of a good thing," Nero used to shout before drowning himself in blood and wine. His sordid conviction about overindulgence turned out to be a rather sublime error in judgment. Now, I needed to exorcise the constant bloodshed and insanity I had lived with during my time with that madman. Watching humans get gored, beheaded, or crucified daily weighs on even us Angels. My long walk, as I called it, led me to the town of Cortina d'Ampezzo.

Cortina sits in a fertile valley in northern Italy, surrounded by prominent sandstone peaks called *Dolomiti*. They rise 10,000 feet above the oceans and, by far, some of my father's best work here on Earth. Far away from Rome and the constant scourge of humanity, I felt an absolute rising inner peace upon walking into the pristine valley. Upon my arrival, I sought out and touched a Roman Centurion by the name of Titus Septimus.

He was the *primus pilus* of the roman generals – the first man into the shit. He commanded thousands of loyal men trained in the way of soldiering and extremely capable of killing. Titus' legionnaires camped out along the shores of lake Santa Croce twenty miles to the south. Primus ordered his legion to spend the month of July recuperating from their recent efforts further north against an upstart new tribe of people he called *Vandals*.

"So, you are the man they call Annaeus Seneca?" Titus asked me. "Are you some kind of teacher?"

"I can be many things, Primus. How can I serve you?" I asked.

"Is it true?"

"Is what true?"

"Don't be foolish. Is Nero dead?" he shouted.

"I can safely report, Primus, that yes, in fact, he has died," I responded.

"I heard Caesar was torn apart by lions. Tell me, teacher, how did you escape that madness?" Titus asked.

"Lucky, I guess, does it matter?"

"I suppose not, teacher," Titus said while scribing on some, what I thought, were insignificant legal documents. "But it begs the question, of course," he led on.

"What question might that be?" I asked.

"Look around you, teacher, what do you see?" he responded, clutching the pen he used for his legal consent. "All of *this* is because of my efforts," he said while waving down the hill.

His marble and sandstone country villa looked and aimed for Etruscan and Greek magnificence. However, compared to the Republic's senators' villas, it was small. Nonetheless, he adopted the Greeks' architectural brilliance to build his magnificent home. The unmistakable architecture and sublime artwork made it so.

"Below you is the valley floor, ripe with grapes and plebes," he declared. "Every plant and animal in this valley belong to me, teacher," he went on to inform me.

"And the plebes, who do they belong to?" I asked.

"They are free to come and go, but they choose to stay and work the land as tenant farmers," he explained. "In exchange for my protection and Rome's, they provide me with all the necessary provisions needed to run my villa and this town."

Titus was a studied architect and war engineer. Before his climb to the top of the Roman hierarchy, he learned warfare and politics. Being brutally clever, as a student Titus stood out like the many statuesque peaks surrounding the valley I had walked through upon my arrival. It was no surprise to learn that while I was playing with Nero, young Titus had systematically enslaved hundreds of people during his many campaigns in Spain and the new Isle of England. The purpose of his enslavement was to acquire men, women, and children to build the *Villa de Primus Septimus.*

"You have built a masterpiece here, Primus. I am thoroughly impressed," I said.

The villa, carved into the hillside above Cortina d'Ampezzo, was magnificent. The town center sat at 4,000 feet, and the highest peaks surrounding the alpine valley rose to over 10,000 feet. Further down the valley at lower elevations, Titus engaged his Portuguese slaves to plant their hearty grapevines, which managed to survive the cold winters and produce exceptional berries in the fall. He also had a small legion of blacksmiths, carpenters, artists, chefs, whores, and other slaves.

The villa had a small atrium due to the seasonal cold and his Centurion budget. Titus added luxurious bedrooms, living rooms, a temple for worship, a large modern kitchen with adjacent food storage, and a large dining room for his occasional guests. All the mosaic floors were designed and built with under-floor central heating, which he called the *hypocaust*. Titus was most proud of his plumbed bathing facilities equipped with piping hot mineral water sourced from the hot spring above the villa.

The entire hillside below the taut villa was terraced and fortified with large iron stakes pointing downhill. Titus flooded the high terraced walls with water from another fresh-water spring in the winter, leaving large sheets of thick vertical ice. When encased by the winter freeze, the ice wall undoubtedly blocked any man from entering his home from November through March. If anyone had thoughts of raiding the compound, one look at the fortress would surely change their thinking.

"Very well, down to business," Titus said, snapping me from my luxurious daydream.

"I need to return to my men and deal with another uprising in Gaul. You will stay here until I return, hopefully by next summer," he stated. "That *is* why you are here? Fleeing the hordes that want you dead?" he surmised.

"Yes, well, that certainly answers your question, doesn't it," I responded.

"Perhaps," he questioned. "I have only one rule, and s*he* is off-limits," he went on to say.

"A rule? Who is off-limits, Titus?" I begged to differ.

"Avelina, my slave girl," he replied. "She will make sure you are well fed and cared for, but you are not to touch her. Do I make myself clear?"

"Of course, Titus, I completely understand," I falsely promised.

Avelina, enslaved by Titus, was new to me. She came from Portugal. She had dark brown hair falling below her waist, green and gold eyes, and soft tan skin color that never faded, even in winter. I cannot say why he left me with her or why it took so long for him to return, until later. I have often thought of her since. It is why I hate horses.

CHAPTER FOUR

66666666666666666666666666666666

AVELINA AND THE VANDALS – 70 CE

Winter comes fast to Cortina, enveloping the valley with harsh cold blankets of snow. Since Titus' departure, I quickly settled into a beautiful, lustful routine. My strange feelings for Avelina felt like a unique, biological magnate. Despite his stern warning, I unexpectedly fell prey to that diabolical feeling you humans all seem to be in search of – love.

"The walls are frozen outside, Annaeus, come back to bed," Avelina said.

When the water fell over the walls, we became encased inside Titus' villa, looking down upon the village below, cocooned within our warm, loving palace. The peaks above occasionally reflected warm light down upon us, but we were always worried about our captor – winter.

"I'm hungry and thirsty. What time is it?" I asked Avelina.

"It's still early," she responded. "Come back to bed."

I suppose it was easy to fall in love with Avelina, despite the perceived threat of punishment from Titus. The physical isolation within an otherwise comfortable accommodation made it only a matter of time, I suppose. But love makes you do strange things. My strong physical attraction to Avelina fed a new personal desire for fleshy pleasure, and it was unstoppable.

"But the sun is shining," I said. "Let's go mingle with the plebes and tour the village today. Besides, Titus has given you plenty of warm clothes to choose from in his absence."

"When do you think he will return? Should I be worried?" she then asked for the first time.

"Why should you be worried?" I responded.

"You know what he will do to me if he finds out?" she said.

"Let's save our worries for another day, shall we, my sweet. Today we live," I told her.

My touch was enough, and Avelina rolled out of bed and smiled.

"Wait then, and let me get ready."

The air was brisk while I waited for Avelina to join me. I looked downhill from the large balcony overlooking the village below as the snow-covered peaks reflected a warm radiance upon us. When she appeared, fully gowned and looking perfect, I choked up and felt a pang in my stomach, which I didn't necessarily understand. We walked down to the village hand in hand. With each snowy step, Avelina pulled my arm into her petite body.

"I know what you are, my love," she said while looking up at me.

"Whatever are you talking about, Lina?" I responded, using my lover's name.

"How long do you have?" she said, squeezing my arm. "Will Astaroth come soon?"

"Who? What are you talking about, my love," I asked, knowing what she meant.

We had just set foot on the snow-crusted dirt road at the bottom of the terraced steps and made our way towards town. She never pushed my response as false or dodgy because I was too indifferent to answer. So, we walked, arm in arm, toward the village of Cortina.

"When did you fall?" she asked.

"Fall, what do you mean?"

"You don't remember me, do you?" she questioned.

"What are you saying, my love?" I responded.

"You are Beelzebub, youngest of three. Before you fell, I was an angel like you," she said.

I stopped us and moved her away, looking into her eyes to confirm her story.

"It's ok, never mind, my love, let's live for today and the next, and time shall tell," she said, letting me off the hook.

I scoured my memory, trying to remember her before my fall, but struggled with the answer. Time is irrelevant for most of us, and we tend to lack shared memories because time is infinite. Angels are created by God. They go through a period of confusion, then are given their wings. We have immaculate immortality. Our strength and power come from our wings. They are what keep us immortal. Without them, we become finite, imperfect, mortal, and ordinary - like humans.

During the time of confusion, we act like children and have heroes that we admire and revere. There have always been good angels and evil angels. Like myself, some angels prefer to be like my personal childhood hero – Loki, god of mischief.

During my time of confusion, Loki's tricks and schemes wreaked havoc across the realms. I pretended to act like Loki, playing tricks on my classmates. Most of the confused, that's what they called us, wanted to be like Thor, god of thunder.

The good angels pretended to wield a hammer, striking down those who would harm humankind. Before we got our wings, the Confused would play "Thor versus Loki" during recess, making pretend lighting and thunder sounds before pouncing on the Lokis. I suppose those childhood beatings subconsciously forced me to forget my time of confusion and, most likely, Avelina.

"Were you a Thor or a Loki?" I asked Avelina to make conversation.

"Thor, of course, I spent most of my time protecting you from the other Thors, especially your brothers," she replied.

After a brief second, we both shared a laugh, making that moment in time perfect.

"What happened to your wings?" I asked.

"Free will, my love," she answered. "I decided I wanted to be free of his rules, so I did the one thing I knew he would never forgive me for," she replied in a quieter voice.

"He punishes us for our slips back into confusion, but he will always forgive," I said. "In time, he will forgive you, Lina, you'll see," I assured her.

"Not me, not ever," she abruptly responded.

"But why? What did you do that is beyond his forgiveness?" I asked.

Avelina began to weep, causing her tears to freeze the lashes below her eyes.

"I killed his unborn child inside me," she said.

I momentarily let go of her hand and stood still in the middle of the village square. I had no response to her betrayal. She was correct, God would never forgive her for such willful and wanton deceit.

"He said I could spend the rest of my days amongst the humans as one of their slaves," she added. "I've been down here ten years, washing Titus' feet and feeding his appetite for flesh and meat and wine. He will never let me go, Beez. I will grow old and ugly and human."

She looked and felt beaten. Truly hopeless. But I didn't care. I felt even stronger pangs of love for Avelina, knowing that she was completely free to love me if Titus stayed away. I compromised that condition within my head, knowing that I could always touch Titus and send him off to his natural-born pastime – war.

I rapidly began to warm, and my heart pounded with such a tremendous pleasurable force, the feeling of which I had never felt before, that I turned red in the face – stretched by my ear to ear smile. How simple yet confusing love felt. Free to not be scared or jealous or alone. A ready supply of energy with every simple kiss. An explosion of physical pleasure at my side and a glorious villa to explore our mutual physical attraction. The confidence one assumes with such a bond, however, can lead to despair when interrupted.

"But now you are with me, and I will bathe you and feed you and make love to you as long as we are together. I still have my wings. Nothing can harm you, my love," I promised her. "We are both free to do what we want." I believed.

I suddenly felt the urge to celebrate the free will Avelina had sacrificed so much for just so that she could feel independent and free from his conditions, rules, and consequences.

"We must celebrate," I joyfully said. "Here are some *denarii*, my love. Go buy yourself some jewelry from the Sicilian. I will get us some of that special bubbling wine from the Italian around the corner. Let's meet for lunch at Giuseppe's when the sun is directly overhead."

Avelina wiped the frozen bits of ice from her eyes and threw both her arms around me - pushing back for a moment to ask for more denarii.

"I want a new dress as well, my love."

"Of course," I said.

We parted ways with the excitement of our future eagerly waiting. Everything was perfect, or so it seemed. The one real weakness or defect of being in love and having free will was ignorance of reality. The other problem with free will is that people and their ideas collide. When more than one person has free will, all hell breaks loose. It was an oversight of mine, believing our newly found free will was unique and defensible. Unfortunately, unbeknownst to me, love can also cloud free will's consequences, exposing lovers to devastating heartache and terrible loss.

"Free will, amongst humans, cannot be trusted," my father said during my confusion. "Left to their own devices for too long, humans will destroy everything good I have created on Earth. Never give them too long a leash, Beez, for they will surely hang themselves with it."

I walked around the corner and down a side street toward Baptiste, the winemaker, still full of love and free will. Nothing would interfere with my newfound happiness.

"*Buon pomeriggio, amico mio, come stai oggi,*" I greeted Baptiste in Italian.

"*Sto bene, insegnante; Cosa possa offrirti, amico mio,*" he replied with a warm embrace.

"*il tuo miglior vino spumeggiante...*some of your finest bubbling wine," I said.

The sun was not quite directly overhead, but it felt like late morning, given the glow coming from the peaks. The icicles were starting to drip and held the promise of dropping. The village was brimming with activity, and people were out, doing their business. The air temperature was brisk, however, and I even saw my breath. I felt comfortable with my judgment of time because I didn't want to keep Avelina waiting by herself. It's always a thing, making sure you are on time, especially when you are in love. Even still, given the perfect conditions, I decided to make small talk with my friend, Baptiste.

We drank many of his different fine wines. I blathered on, mainly about the weather and beautiful women and the snow. He shared with me his *Riserva Speciale*, which was divine. After drinking it, I felt stupid and happy, so I purchased several gallons of Baptiste's wine. I immediately planned in my head to let the wine sit in Titus' cold cellar, then drink it like water with Avelina. I determined that with so much free will and the benefit of love, I would lay about with Avelina during the warm summer days to come and get sleepy drunk on Baptiste's wine. Everything was going to be great. Life was going to be perfect.

· · · · · · · · · ·

As I slugged down another glass of his *Riserva*, the expression on Baptiste's face changed from happy to stone. He opened his left hand and dropped the carafe of special red wine he was holding. His eyes showed fear, and his body trembled. Behind me emerged a giant man with long blond braided hair, cold blue eyes, and a thick red beard from out on the main street. He was sitting on the back of an even more giant horse, adorned with protective metal chains and thick leather. His immense presence just froze Baptiste where he stood.

"What is it, my friend? Who is that man?" I asked.

Baptiste was only capable of a one-word response.

"Vandili."

As I turned to face the man, his arrow glanced my ear before plunging directly through Baptiste's right eye and out the back of his skull, leaving four inches of black feathers sticking out of his new face. Two feet of the arrow stood still, out the back of his head. I stared into his remaining open left eye for a brief second before he collapsed to the ground, face first, pushing the black feathers back into and through his brain.

The Vandals were a wandering tribe of Germanic people known for their brutality in waging war. They were also famous for their skill in training horses for warfare. The Vandals' one absolute pleasure was roaring into towns and villages on horseback to riot, loot, pillage, and destroy people's property. Staring at my dead friend, I was determined to exact painful revenge for such vandalism.

As I marched back onto the main street, I faced hundreds of these giant men on their huge horses. Extending my hands straight out in front, I began to wand them off their horses with my divine power of intervention. By clenching my hands into fists, I crushed their skulls. With each wand left and wand right, the Vandal soldiers began to litter the streets of Cortina. My rage was unstoppable as the blond-haired bodies piled up. And then I heard her cry for help.

"Beez, help me, I'm scared," she shouted. "Please, I don't want to die this way."

Avelina was clinging to a thick wooden post holding up Giuseppe's awning.

"Don't move, I'll come to you," I shouted back. "Wait there."

As I began working my way toward Avelina, she gave up her position behind the wooden post and started running for me. The Vandal hordes were also running for me. The more soldiers I killed, however, did not have the same effect on their well-trained horses. My divine power did not affect those strong-minded beasts, so they just kept charging at full speed toward Avelina and me.

"Go back, wait," I begged. "Avelina, get down," I might have said.

Avelina was first hit by the massive chest of the stampeding Vandal warhorse, flattening her to the ground and knocking her unconscious. Another horse, running empty in the opposite direction, managed to clip her head with his hard hoof, spinning her around and splitting her forehead open. Lying in the middle of the street, she still appeared to have some life left in her body, but I couldn't be sure.

"Avelina!" I cried out while breaking into a mad dash.

More Vandals then began to line up in rows further down the road on the outskirts of town. I would kill them all, I determined.

Not being aware of anything else but Avelina and the Vandals, I failed to account for the remaining riderless horses terrorizing the streets behind me. The Vandals then blew into some large horn that let out a deep moan.

"Arrroooah."

In response, by signaling their retreat, one of their immune horses struck me from behind on his way out of town, leaving me very shaken. As I got to my knees, another horse stepped on top of Avelina's spine, leaving her limp and lifeless. Before I could get to her, an arrow fell from the sky, landing in the back of her neck, killing her instantly.

The king of the Vandals then appeared through his parting ranks. He was giant and blond.

"Your father asked me to send you a message," the king said. "Nothing is for certain, boy. There is no such thing as free will!" he finished.

The Vandal tribe turned and slowly walked off back down the valley. I slumped to the ground, holding Avelina's dead body in my lap. A lone horse walked up behind me, naying, limping and jerking her funny-looking head up and down. The beast seemed to show some remorse or guilt by association, as she lowered her beautiful nose and powerful jaw over Avelina, snorting and grunting her contrition.

"Why, why her?" I asked the horse.

But the beast just dragged her right hoof back, then nodded up and down. She had been speared well enough by one of the villagers – certain to die.

"Merrrhah, merrrrhah," she responded, then proudly walked down the main street, fell to her knees, rolled over, and died.

Little did I know, but my father gave the horse a pass. The Equine, as he called them, are bigger and stronger than any man. My father gave the Equines their strength as a joke, strictly speaking, for his pleasure. Watching the great beast break human bodies was his breakfast. Horses have wit and talent and loved to humiliate men at their forceful discretion. I do enjoy watching them break men's bones.

The Vandals, naturally, knew this about horses and fashioned their dominance and propensity for Hijinx so that they could pillage and plunder villages. They were not necessarily horsing around or whispering per se, but instead had been given the gift of knowledge by my father to help level the playing field with the Romans when relations soured.

I always suspected the Vandals knew about the horse's immaculate beauty, strength, occasional compassion, and immunity from my divine touch. I was made ignorant of that fact during my confusion. The constant fighting with my brothers bled my memory. But now I know. The horse is finicky, intelligent, demanding, robust, and able.

The horse also killed the only worldly love I have ever known.

As I watched the Vandals slowly march out of town on the backs of my new nemesis, I determined to find the animal's weakness, besides the spear. The beast had vanquished my free will and taken my lover, leaving me, once again, with a newfound interest in bloodshed and hatred of horses.

CHAPTER FIVE

6666666666666666666666666666666666

AFTER AVELINA

Since Avelina's death, I have touched many souls over the years.

Attila the Hun, Genghis Khan, and Vlad Prince of Wallachia were bloodthirsty men. Tsar Ivan the Terrible invented the torture chamber with my help. King Leopold II of Belgium loved to terrorize the Congolese to satisfy his greed.

More recently, during the French Revolution, the lawyer Maximilien Robespierre made joyful use of a devilish toy I invented, which he called the *guillotine*. Of course, who can forget my good friends Joe Stalin and his adversary Adolf Hitler? They took a page from Nero's playbook and mechanized mass murder.

I even spent some time in the Cambodian countryside with Pol Pot, where he planted the fields with millions of his people to reeducate them. It seems humans who become authoritarian dictators or fascists like to eliminate smart people and pander to the ignorant masses.

Presently, I have a sudden desire for less violent and bloodthirsty pursuits. As whimsical a notion it may be, I am inclined to share the story of my latest pupil, whether he knows it or not. You see, one of my first orders of business before touching a soul is to erase their memory, which gives me a clean slate. If they have soulmates, then I erase their memory as well.

The one thing that I fear is true love. That can get in the way of my fun and jolt old memories back to life.

There is a true joy in human misfortune that satisfies my need to do evil. I find it very entertaining. Any state of affairs or an event that is deliberately contrary to what you may expect is often amusing and a cause I will always celebrate.

I first touched him in the summer of 2009 as he lay passed out on my couch. He was just so lovable and pathetic, and I needed a break from all the evil men can do. I was living in San Francisco with a serial killer you call the *Zodiac*. For years, he lived amongst you and even held a public office. In the end, he died by the negligence of a drunk driver and I got his luxurious apartment. Some of you even mourned his passing, not knowing the truth.

Nonetheless, since then, I've had an epiphany of sorts. Instead of bloodshed, death, destruction, and horror, I decided it would be fun to use human character flaws and irony for my entertainment. Of course, some bloodshed is unavoidable.

His name is Richard Hardens Daily, and, as I said, he is one wonderfully pathetic fuck up.

CHAPTER SIX

666666666666666666666666666666666

Dog Shit In San Francisco – Summer 2019

He spends most of his days looking for a job, but he's not very successful. His real skill is drinking, doing drugs, and being a *fuck up* as you humans say. That's probably my fault.

Richard likes to sleep on my couch when he stays up late at night. That way, he doesn't have to make the bed. Not that he would.

Today started out promising for him; I mean it. But the whole thing fell apart after he stepped in dog shit on the way to his new job interview with Delores Spatchcock.

Delores is the managing partner at *Wiesel, Sticket & Tooum*, a San Francisco law firm registered to lobby Congress, the White House, and the federal government on behalf of foreign governments. They do a booming business, filing the necessary paperwork with the Department of Justice to comply with the Foreign Agents Registration Act on behalf of shady individuals who want the President's ear or to get rich from wealthy Russian oligarchs that want to influence political activities in the United States. So I convinced Richard that he would be the perfect fit. But, in truth, I just wanted access to some Russian oligarchs to touch and influence.

Anyway, on his way to Delores' office, Richard purchased a cup of burnt coffee. He was hungover with a vicious headache because of the wine he drank the night before. I gave him two pain pills to drink with his coffee, which he chased down with a mini bottle of *Jack Daniels*. I love that shit, and so does Richard. Sometimes we would pour the whiskey straight into the coffee when no one was looking. I was feeling pretty good after, and so was Richard. His meeting with Delores was scheduled for 10:00 am.

"Hurry up, I can't be late again," he said to me.

Everyone is in a hurry at that time of day in San Francisco. It's funny watching humans scatter about, driven by greed or lust or necessity. For example, I watched an old Asian woman try and catch a cable car. At first, she grabbed a hold of the old wooden handle laced with brass or copper; I didn't know which. Nonetheless, it was great because she got dragged through the intersection of California and Kearny streets for about ten yards before she let go of the old wooden handle. I know that doesn't sound very pleasant, but I had to laugh. After, she was helped up by two obese women, probably in their forties. They both fell on top of the old Asian woman. Laughing, I watched them bend over and try to pick her up with no success — what a hilarious spectacle.

"Should we see if they're ok or maybe help them?" Richard asked.

"Don't be stupid, you're already late," I abruptly responded. "Besides, being fat and stupid is no excuse."

By then, two young San Francisco police officers stopped traffic and escorted the old Asian woman and the two fat forty-somethings to the sidewalk. What a lovely mess.

Meanwhile, I wasn't paying attention to where Richard was walking, and neither was he because of the debacle taking place in the busiest intersection in San Francisco at the busiest time of day. That's when he bumped into a woman dressed in all white, carrying a white briefcase. Richard's coffee splashed all over his one clean white work shirt and her pants. She was immediately pissed off at him, which made me happy.

"Watch where you are going, ya drunk asshole," she shouted at him.

Usually, Richard would have responded to her mean-spirited instruction with a few choice words of his own like, "go fuck yourself, lady," but she had stunned him with the *drunk asshole* comment. His pores had betrayed his habit.

As I said, he was in a hurry, so Richard just kept walking and wiping the coffee off his one clean shirt. And that's when it happened.

Bad things usually happen when you are distracted or upset or confused. However, Richard wasn't agitated in any of those ways. In fact, we both were still laughing inside about the old Asian lady and the two fat women tripping over each other in the middle of the busiest street in San Francisco. The entire spectacle was as funny as a well-placed fart. Maybe even funnier.

The truth is, when a stranger labels you a *drunk asshole*, it weighs on you. It felt unfair and slightly inaccurate. I mean, sure, Richard had been drunk the night before, but that wasn't his fault. He met up with some old law school buddies, and one of them, Aaron Fisk, put his card behind the bar and said, "drinks are on me, boys."

Aaron Fisk was a genuine douche bag and liked to throw money around to acquire friends. Richard didn't like him either, so he kept ordering as many drinks as he wanted or needed – I didn't know which. Just because he was drinking two for every one of theirs doesn't make him a bad guy, does it?

Anyway, being distracted or confused or upset, Richard wasn't watching where he was going. After his collision with the white bitch, he swerved into the street, walked along Montgomery street for two or three delivery truck lengths, and then decided to step back onto the curb. A young tree was planted in a hole, encircled by a metal grate, where he stepped back onto the curb. Richard grabbed the tree and hoisted himself between two other fast-walking, busy-minded people to not disrupt people's flow.

As Richard touched down onto the sidewalk, his right foot landed in a great big, steaming fresh pile of dog shit. It was so new that his foot slipped forward, causing him to fall to his left knee and let go of his old leather briefcase. As Richard's momentum carried him onto the sidewalk, his right hand automatically extended out and down to stop his fall. The first thing Richard's hand touched was the skid-marked streak of dog shit left behind by his encased right shoe.

Once his bare hand hit the smelly dog shit, he naturally reacted and pulled his right hand up, causing him to lose his balance and fall sideways onto his right side. The first thing to hit the ground was his right pant leg, rolling over and through the original pile of dog shit. As I tried to pick Richard up, his left shoe slipped on a second, smaller piece of dog shit. As Richard's left foot slipped backward, his left knee went down hard again on more dog shit, then ripped a small hole in his suit. Before I could gather him up, he had dog shit on his right hand, right pant leg, and left knee – which had a hole torn in the middle. It was beautiful.

I retreated with Richard to the small tree and strongly suggested he scrape off the dog shit stuck to his shoe on the metal grate encircling the tree, then use the door handle of the delivery truck parked in the yellow zone to clean the other dog mess off his hand. Unfortunately, there was not much I could do about the hole in his suit, so he just covered it up with his tattered briefcase.

Fortunately, Richard had arrived at his destination five minutes early, so he decided to find a bathroom and clean up the best he could under the circumstances. Just then, however, the same lady dressed in an all-white pantsuit walked by and expressed herself again.

"Karma is a bitch, isn't it," she said without stopping.

At that point, the whiskey, coffee, and pain pills had kicked in, so Richard was free of any inhibition.

"Oh, go fuck yourself, you frog-assed excuse for a whore," he screamed out loud while raising his middle finger.

"Good one," I said in support.

The white bitch, as I call her, just kept on strolling into the building where Richard was having his interview. She never looked back but kept her middle finger raised appropriately high with her back turned.

Richard quickly hurried into the building after he noticed some burly-looking guys heading toward the truck where he had rubbed some of the dog shit off onto their passenger side door handle. Before I followed Richard into the building, I watched the bulky goateed passenger grab the door handle and mash the discarded remains of fresh dog shit between his knuckles.

"Ah, what the fuck?" he said to my delight.

Meanwhile, Richard was able to find a bathroom in the building's lobby and wash his hands and suit. I was sure he removed most of the dog shit from his shoes before heading to the twenty-sixth floor. Richard's job interview with one of the senior partners looked promising before that.

"Richard Daily for Miss Spatchcock, please," he said to the receptionist.

She had big tits and probably smoked, but that didn't make her friendly.

"Have a seat; I will let her know you are here," is all she said.

I walked over to the leather chair opposite a small table standing on an expensive Persian rug. Richard followed me. After a few brief seconds, the unmistakable smell of dog shit started wafting up from his feet. He lifted each shoe sideways and found there was still plenty of fresh dog shit wedged into the cracks of the heels and in the tread of his soles. Panic set in as the smell of highly potent dog shit filled the entire reception room. Something about dog shit wrangles with the olfactory: the receptionist even stood up and walked out of the room, covering her nostrils with her cupped hand. The look on her face was priceless.

Even better, Richard was all alone, except for me, wearing a torn suit and smelling of overwhelmingly rancid dog shit. That's when the senior partner, Delores Spatchcock, entered the room. As she was about to introduce herself, Richard had yet to lift his head.

"Mr. Daily, I'm Delores..."

She stopped short of finishing her full name when she saw his face.

It was the White Bitch.

"Richard? I thought it was you," she said. "Now, kindly and as fast as possible, see yourself out and take your dog shit shoes with you!"

Our day was just beginning, so I encouraged Richard to wipe as much dog shit off on her Persian rug as possible before we started to drink.

CHAPTER SEVEN

6666666666666666666666666666666

THE EFFECTS OF DRUGS
AND ALCOHOL

It wasn't difficult to convince Richard to eat another pain pill and walk to our favorite dungy dive bar that opens at 6 a.m. as most of them do.

Scooter Rebock's serves four-dollar martinis and provides popcorn for its patrons. Despite the dark, low light, and moldy smell, *Rebock's* hosts mostly well-to-do white guys. There was Larry George, a stockbroker, who had been perched at the bar since it opened. He recently gambled away his 14-year-old daughter's college fund with no way of replacing the $100,000. Then there was Antoinette Archambault, the bartender. She had tattoos inked all over her arms and neck, a tongue bolt and nipple rings. She was nice to Richard. Her French father named her Antoinette, but she went by Tony.

"It's nice to see a friendly face," Richard said while hanging his tattered old briefcase on the hook under the bar.

"What are you having, loser?" Tony replied in an upbeat, soulful voice.

"The special," he answered and placed two twenties and a ten on the counter.

The *special* was a couple of cheap martinis and a bindle of about a half-gram of stomped on cocaine. Richard would need the "pick me up" after his morning failures.

I cannot feel the effects of such a wasteful drug, but I always encouraged Richard to order the special. It always made him drink more, which naturally made him buy more of Tony's white powder.

"Let's have some fun this afternoon, gorgeous, my treat," Richard began, as the cocaine-fueled arrogance and know-it-all banter drove his confidence.

He worked on Tony for the past three weeks and believed he was closer to wearing her down with his bullshit. Richard habitually lied about his success, wealth, and general station in life after a few bathroom visits. Although he was well-educated and intelligent, he remained stuck on the Sisyphean task of swooning Tony, which was enormously entertaining. Today would be no different, and Tony would see through his futile charade.

"I don't date losers, babe, and my boyfriend wouldn't appreciate it either," she explained in a somewhat public fashion. I love watching Richard get rejected.

"One day, you will change your mind," Richard proudly disagreed. "I doubt it, honey, but credit for trying," she replied with a smile.

As I said, Tony was adorned with many piercings in most of her private and semi-public parts. She liked to stick her tongue out to prove that fact, which encouraged Richard to ask for more intimate viewing. She once pulled her top down and exposed her bare nipple rings and big breasts to him, which convinced Richard he was succeeding.

She applied her professional trade as a bartender, enabling poor Richard to buy more drinks. After one hour at Scooter Rebock's, Tony had sold him two specials, a pint of lager, and a shot of tequila. Given his newfound confidence, Richard would leave two twenties on the bar and forget about them within minutes. Richard started the day with three twenty's, two tens', and a fifty-dollar bill in his wallet. Given his drug and alcohol abuse, he was down to zero dollars and little common sense.

Fortunately, things were about to get worse.

CHAPTER EIGHT
6666666666666666666666666666666666
BEING OVERCONFIDENT
WITH A FART

If nothing else, Richard knew when to cut his losses and move on with his day. That's when Larry George started bemoaning his circumstances to him.

"Rich, you wanna know the secret to happiness?" he asked.

"Oh, by all means, Larry, do tell us," Richard facetiously replied.

"Try not to be a dumb asshole," was his pearl of wisdom.

"Well, that certainly is a good start," Richard offhandedly responded. "You seem down, partner; what's giving you the shits? It can't be as bad as it seems."

But it was.

Larry had developed a pretty good habit for Tony's specials after suffering a string of gambling losses. He was upside down with his bookie for over $50,000, and the sharks were circling. That's when he decided to place more of his daughter's college fund on a few "sure things," which I made sure would fail. The more money he bet to cover his mounting losses, a jump shot would hit the front rim, or an otherwise catchable pass would get dropped in the endzone. It was hilarious.

"I'm in deep with the Scattuzzo brothers, Rich, and today is the day," he said.

"For what? Can't you work something out with them?" Richard asked.

"They have been carrying me for two months, and I can't ask my wife to bail me out again. She thinks I stopped betting years ago," Larry responded.

"Tell ya what, let's grab a piss, get you fixed up, and I'll buy lunch – we both could use some food," Richard offered.

The two losers then strolled into the men's room - a single toilet behind a locking door. Naturally, Richard dipped his car key into the bag and took a sniff. He then scooped up another bump and held the key under Larry's nose.

"This will fix you up," Richard said after rubbing his nose.

"One more," Larry recklessly demanded.

The cocaine was undoubtedly mixed with baby laxatives. Nevertheless, the thought of doing a snort of cocaine gave Larry the inevitable urge to shit. He believed he could relieve the innate calling with a careful fart. But his overconfidence with the fart was somewhat mistaken and, ultimately, foolhardy.

"Jesus, that sounded pretty wet, Larry," Richard surmised. "Ahh, dude, that's so fucking foul," he subsequently complained. "God knows that's gonna itch when it dries."

Larry had completely shat in his pants, which left both men in a rather smelly bind.

"I'm gonna let you clean up, partner; use your underwear and meet me outside," Richard instructed.

"Where should I leave them after?" Larry asked as both men broke down with laughter.

"Don't leave them in here, man; Tony will flip out and 86 us for life," Richard determined. "Wrap that foul shit in an ass gasket and put it in your coat pocket; we'll dump it in the trash outside," he advised.

Larry followed Richard's instruction, and the two men did their best to walk out of the dark bar casually – it was 2:30 in the afternoon.

"Alright, my love, time for lunch," Richard said, then leaned over the bar to steal a kiss from Tony.

"You idiots be safe and come back soon," she replied. "Take care of yourself, Larry," Tony added, sensing his impending doom.

Larry was too hopped up on the double bump and somewhat paranoid about the shit-stained *tighty-whities* concealed in his coat, so he forced a smile and walked on by the lovely Antoinette.

"Where to now?" Richard asked Larry outside in broad daylight.

"One of my partners has a nice high-rise apartment over on Beale Street. He's out of town. Let's grab a burrito at *El Mono Cantor* and head over there; I want to show you something."

Sniff.

CHAPTER NINE

6666666666666666666666666666666666

BEELZEBUB'S LOYAL FRIENDS

Humans have so many ways to suffer, feel anguish, and despair. In Larry's case, he was convinced of his impending doom, having no way out – a form of grief. The inability to see beyond what is right in front of you, it seems, is just another form of human suffering, which was mildly entertaining. Even I was guilty of not seeing the obvious. As Richard and Larry marched down market street, Larry began to ramble on about one of my natural enemies, the Peregrine falcon.

"Did you know the Peregrine falcon is the fastest animal on Earth," Larry informed Richard as they strolled down Market Street toward Beale Street.

"I thought the cheetah was; don't they run like 70 miles an hour?" Richard replied.

"Nope, not even close," explained Larry.

"Why in the fuck are you telling me this; who gives a shit anyway?" Richard asked.

"My partner says there is a nesting pair on the roof of his building," explained Larry.

As it turned out, the pair had a clutch of four, and three were getting ready to take their first leap of faith off the rooftop. The runt was not going to make it. Nonetheless, it was always tricky for fledglings, given all the skyscrapers with glass windows and my many associates – the crows.

I occasionally joined them in their sporting effort to attack them in mid-flight. However, the exercise was primarily for my entertainment because the crows were nothing more than a nuisance to the Peregrines - they could hit speeds of 240 mph in an instant, leaving the bothersome crows to their murder.

Occasionally, a fledgling would confusingly fly into a shiny skyscraper and plunge to its death, feeding the lowly pigeons and seagulls.

"No shit, can we get on the roof from his floor?" Richard asked with some excitement.

"I think that might be my only option," replied Larry somewhat unresponsively.

"What are you talking about?" Richard naturally asked.

"Nothing, forget it; let's just get those burritos and head on up."

The luxury apartment building was 20 stories tall, and Larry's partner owned the penthouse.

"Make yourself comfortable, Richie; plates are above the kitchen counter," Larry said, then started removing various items from his jacket pockets – keys, sunglasses, betting notes, and his wallet. He left them on the credenza next to the dining room table.

"Do you think they were following us?" Larry asked. But Richard didn't hear him.

I quickly realized that Larry was susceptible to my touch after tossing his coat over the couch and walking onto the balcony. Little did he know the fledglings were looking down from the safety of their rooftop perch, getting ready to jump. Right behind the newcomers were the crows.

"How do we get to the roof?" Richard asked Larry.

"Out the front door, to the right, and up the stairs," he responded. "I'll see you up there."

I stayed behind with Larry, unable to stop myself. It didn't take much: just a deep breath and a dive-bombing crow.

"What the fuck?" he said while kicking and punching my black beauties away. They are my most loyal soldiers – the crows.

As the fledglings took their maiden leap of faith, one by one, their conceited parents watched from above, fighting off the delightful shenanigans of my playful pets. All the while, Larry scrambled and jerked his way toward the ledge, warding off the attack from my associates.

"Get off me," he shouted while they kept diving at his head.

Meanwhile, the aerial acrobats, my sworn enemies, were diving just out of reach.

Larry thrashed and flailed his arms in a rather violent, desperate attempt to ward off my feathered cohorts as he stumbled toward the edge. But before I could intervene, Larry tripped on one of his partner's potted plants and lost his balance. With his unfortunate momentum and gravity being what it is, Larry catapulted over the balcony and plunged to a rather messy demise.

Oops.

CHAPTER TEN

6666666666666666666666666666666666

WHAT ARE THE ODDS?

On September 7, 2019, Larry placed a $10,000 bet with Mario Scattuzzo that the Baltimore Ravens would cover a 7-point spread and beat the Miami Dolphins in their own home. At the time, it wasn't that covering the spread was such a fanciful wager given the fact that the visiting Ravens had Lamar Jackson at the helm, but rather, Larry used a specific stake called "points betting," which is typically a very risky bet.

"Give me points away on the Ravens, Mario," Larry said over the phone. "Ten thousand, I'm good for it."

The way it works is once the spread is covered, a better makes 1x the wager per point away from the spread. On this day, the maximum Larry could win or lose was set at $200,000. So, if the Ravens won by 26 or more, Larry would win $200,000. Similarly, if the Ravens lost by 26 or more, Larry would lose $200,000. The Ravens won 59-10.

I watched Larry tumble over the glass railing and hit a terminal velocity of 150 mph before exploding all over the sidewalk below. His body liquified upon impact, spraying the local hot dog man with guts and shit and brains. I hadn't seen such gore and violence since my days with Nero.

"Hey, the birds are jumping off the building, man. It's pretty fucking cool," Richard said. "Where is Larry?"

"Ah, he had an accident," was the best I could come up with at that moment.

"What do you mean, he had an accident; where is he?"

"Very unexpected," I muttered. "But I think it's best if we leave now."

"What are you talking about, man? All of his stuff is still here; what the fuck happened?"

"Well, since you ask, he was walking out on the balcony, then tripped over that flowerpot," I explained, leaving out the bit about the crows.

"Yeah, and then what?"

"He fell," I said.

"He fell?" Richard repeated my answer. "Where, where did he fall?"

"Over," I said while pointing to the glass railing. "But I do think we should be on our way under the circumstances."

Richard slowly walked out onto the balcony and peered over the glass railing. The crowds of shocked pedestrians were already frozen with their mouths covered. Groups of two and three were awkwardly holding each other while others were somewhat frantic, especially the hot dog man – covered with bits and pieces of Larry.

"Oh my god, what the hell," Richard said with his hands clasped behind his head.

After some nervous reflection and pacing, Richard tried to do the right thing.

"We should probably give the cops or somebody a statement and explain what happened," Richard suggested.

"Do you think that is wise, in your condition?" I offered. "We don't know the owner, and Larry may not have had his permission to be here. You saw his condition. I'm not a judge, but what if they take your blood? What will you tell them anyway?"

"I don't know, the truth, it was an accident, right?"

"Why leave it to chance?" I persisted. "You're intoxicated Richard, Larry is the last man you were with. Are you certain you want to get involved?"

As luck would have it, just when Richard was about to make the wrong decision and tell the truth, Larry's paranoia proved to be accurate. Call it fate or dumb luck, but Mario Scattuzzo had been following us from Scooter Rebocks.

"Yo, Larry, youz lucky son of a bitch, it's Mario," he said. "Knock, knock, anybody here?"

Mario was a prideful bookie. Even in defeat, "*Scattuzzo always pays on time*" was his motto. So after Larry placed his final bet with the Scattuzzos, Mario wrote a note, as he always did, on a small notepad and gave it to Larry.

LG: 10k fazools – Ravens -7, 1x points away.

The note was sitting on the credenza along with the remainder of Larry's knick-knacks.

"He's in a meeting; how can we help you?" I quickly asked Mario.

"I got some business with Larry. Who da fuck are youz guys?" he asked rather thickly.

"Larry's associates," I responded.

Mario Scattuzzo was the younger brother of Dante Scattuzzo. Another lovable loser who happened to be in the wrong place at the right time. A perfect patsy or *zimbello,* as the Italians like to say.

"He asked us to collect the winnings for the Raven's game and left your note on the credenza," I informed him with a touch. "Can I offer you a beer?"

"Ah, yeah, sure, why not," Mario obediently responded.

I poured the beer into a glass to collect his fingerprints.

"So, when will he be back? I think I should pay Larry, minus what he owes us, of course," he said.

"It's going to be a while, my friend, an important meeting with the boss. But as I said, he told us to collect the difference," I falsely assured him.

Mario had a dull wit and gullible nature, so it didn't take much to convince him to leave the money. After two or three beers and one of Richard's bumps, Mario had left his mark on several glasses and the kitchen counter as well. Unfortunately, Mario pocketed the marker before he left.

"Ciao, my friend," Richard blurted out before closing the front door.

"Let's see what Mario has left us," I said.

As you can imagine, and much to my surprise, Mario left behind $150,000 in nicely wrapped hundreds. What a wonderful sack of fun.

"Wholly shit and mother of God," Richard slowly announced after pouring the loot onto the glass table. "What are we supposed to do with this?"

And just like that, my days with Nero jumped back into my memory, reinvigorating my designs to play with Richard's human character flaws.

"We can start with new suits, then find a nice penthouse to indulge ourselves in the finest luxuries money can buy," I told him.

"But shouldn't we…." Richard started to ask.

All he needed was a quick touch, and his morals and better judgment evaporated as we grabbed the money, wiped our prints, and headed out the door for some champagne, new clothes, and whatever else we could buy with poor, dead Larry George's winnings.

Our night was just beginning.

CHAPTER ELEVEN
6666666666666666666666666666666666

MONEY: THE ROOT OF ALL EVIL

My greatest weapon has always been deception. By coating my lies in a veneer of truth, it became much more comfortable to fool Richard into accepting what is false. Such sophistry worked well on him. Deep down inside, he was too nice, always ready to expose his willingness to provide himself with the things he desired. Humans take and consume each other, often quibbling over ridiculous and unimportant trivialities. It's a uniquely human character flaw. Even Richard, despite being a fuck-up, was downright brilliant, but fell victim to the lure of frivolity. My fallacious arguments convinced him that evil is good, dark is light, and what is wrong is right.

Money, of course, is the root of all evil and constantly changes people. First and foremost, it makes them greedy, arrogant, and foolish. I've even seen people get upset – over money.

The death of Larry weighed on Richard, but our sack of cash proved more effective at relieving his perceived *emotional pain* – whatever that is.

"I still smell like shit," he said to me. "And my suit is ripped."

Our first stop was a cheap sporting goods store, where I purchased an *Ironman* backpack to conceal the cash better. Who would ever imagine a kid carrying that much cash? The second stop was the Four Seasons Hotel on Market Street.

With *our* winnings, we booked the Presidential suite and added two adjacent rooms.

"Time to toss these rags out and soak in the bath," Richard said while hastily removing his clothing. "Crack open some wine, call Tony, and invite her up…tell her to bring some friends."

The excitement of wealth makes impulse spending a rapid response. Within minutes, I had ordered thousands of dollars worth of food, booze, and wine to be delivered to our suite. The concierge, Mr. Chang, was on speed dial, organizing a mobile suit maker, musicians, playful women, and more inquiries into drugs and alcohol. A thousand-dollar tip kept his confidence in our rapidly expanding debauchery. He even organized the service elevator to be used as our back-door entrance.

By 8 pm, we were both wholly refitted with handsome Italian suits, two street musicians playing some mashup of jazz and rock, cases of fine wine, bottles of champagne, three kinds of hard liquor, five strippers, and a large salad bowl full of cocaine.

By 10 o'clock, the party was out of bounds.

All the strippers were half-naked and turning tricks in the adjacent rooms and spacious bathrooms with the hotel staff. Even Mr. Chang fell prey to the lure of drugs, alcohol, and sex. He started running around the suite in his underwear with his tie around his head, pretending to be John Rambo.

Kitchen staff, bellhops, maids, and security officers were all downing shrimp dumplings, snorting cocaine, and slugging expensive bottles of wine and liquor. Everybody was dancing or just jumping up and down to the beat of the street musicians' tunes. Anyone who entered the suite became susceptible to my touch and let loose their primordial need to eat, drink, snort, and fuck. And leading them all was big Rich Daily.

We spent nearly 30,000 dollars before midnight. Richard locked most of the cash in the room safe but was still slinging hundred-dollar bills at each one of his whimsical, drug-fueled desires well into the night. When he felt tired, he would take a snort. If he felt wired, Richard would gulp down a shot of tequila or glass of wine. When he felt manly, he would throw his arm around one of the strippers and take her into the master bedroom. If he couldn't perform, Richard would eat some Viagra. Each time Richard ran low on cash, he would sneak into the master bedroom and take out another $1,000 and repeat the tirade for several more hours.

By 2 am, with my help, strangers of all makes and models showed up and immediately joined the drug-fueled melee. Dancing and sex would devolve into loud banter and hero stories. Once the music started up again, and the bodies started gyrating, the nudity and sex would overwhelm the partygoers. By this time, Richard lost track of time, reality, and necessarily who he thought he was.

It was comical.

"Are you royalty or something?" one ditzy stripper asked him.

"Yes, something like that," he replied through his locked jaw.

During the drunken soiree's height, Richard jumped up and down on one of the couches, barely dressed. It was the perfect opportunity to add some brief madness to the gathering. I couldn't help myself, so as he launched himself into the air, I moved some molecules, sending him airborne towards the large glass dining room table.

Richard came crashing down onto the table, shattering right through it, ending up slumped between the metal frame parts. The semi-thick shards of glass carved him up pretty good, leaving him bloodied from several large and deep lacerations on his butt cheeks and left arm. The mood and the room went instantly quiet.

Mr. Chang was the first person to come to his senses, seeing the carnage from the evening's events.

"Mr. Richard, you ok?" he asked.

"I'm not sure; I don't think so, although I don't know," Richard muttered.

"This not good, Mr. Richard, you bleed all over my carpet, not good," he replied.

Once the blood started leaking from his ass cheeks, the partygoers started fleeing the suite like proverbial rats on a sinking ship. I instinctively pushed more molecules during the exodus, causing half-dressed strippers to roll their ankles and tumble to the floor. The four-body pile-up was made even more entertaining by the girls slipping and sliding on top of each other as they attempted to get to their feet on the champagne-drenched tile floor. Then, as they drunkenly used each other as props to get to their feet, clothes started tearing off, causing one of the girls to throw the first blow.

"Get off me, bitch," one said

"That's mine," another yelled.

Just as those two were working out their differences, another grabbed ahold of Amber's handbag to get to her feet. The purse, fortunately, was half open and cheaply slung over her shoulder. As Tiffany pulled down on the bag to hoist herself up, her weight could not be supported by the chintzy straps and they snapped, catapulting her back into the dining room. Tiffany's momentum carried her past Mr. Chang, where she eventually tripped over a lone sneaker and fell over the metal table frame into the pile of broken glass and right on top of Richard's head

– pounding it back into the chards of glass and rendering him unconscious. Tiffany was now bloodied and confused.

Amber, of course, had been fleecing Richard for hours. Her cheap handbag was stuffed with about 15 or 20 hundred-dollar bills when Tiffany ripped it open, sending the wad of ill-gotten gains into the air above the mosh pit of fleeing strippers, street persons, bellhops, and maids. After three seconds of stunned silence, the partygoers went berserk, scrambling to gather up the cash. Fistfights, catfights, wrestling matches, and tug-o-wars instantly broke out as they each scrambled for a share of the money.

Tiffany fought off Angelica. Manny wrestled with Dante. Edgar punched Letitia. One after another, they kept fighting and struggling and slipping and falling over each other while they grabbed the hundred-dollar bills and wadded them into their pockets or pouches. For the first time in a very long time, I sat back and enjoyed a booming, gut-wrenching laugh. But, of course, the entertainment could not last forever, or so I thought.

As I enjoyed my work, Mr. Chang suddenly came running into the room armed with a red fire extinguisher and fired its white foam all over the strippers and hotel staff.

"You motha fuckas gonna leave now!" he shouted. "No more fucky business."

The white foam covered the floor as Mr. Chang forced the greedy lot further out the front door with every blast. Those temporarily blinded by the agent received two or three firm kicks in the ass and further instruction from Mr. Chang.

"Get, go now!" he shouted, using the red fire extinguisher as a cattle prod of sorts.

After what seemed like several minutes, most of the partygoers had left and the room was nearly empty. Richard was just regaining his consciousness when Mr. Chang sat down next to him, smashing his face into his hands, and began to weep uncontrollably.

"What happened? Is that my blood? What in God's name did you do, Mr. Chang?"

"What I do? What I do?" Mr. Chang responded in confusion. "Fuck you, Mr. Richard, you do all this. You fuck me up real good, lose job," Chang screamed.

Looking around the room, I knew that my work was complete. After tonight, Mr. Chang would surely lose his job, and Richard was probably going to jail. To my surprise, however, that's not what happened.

"How bad am I bleeding?" asked Richard. "Can you get someone up here that can patch me up?"

"Why should I help you, you fucking fuck," Mr. Chang responded.

Richard appeared to sober up a bit and made his way into the bathroom, where he grabbed two nice soft white monogrammed towels and immediately saturated them with his blood.

"Look, I can fix this, but we're gonna need some help," Richard offered. "Can we get two or three cleaning ladies up here? I know a glass guy who can have this table fixed in an hour."

"New shift start at 10 am, that's less than two hours," Mr. Chang pointed out in a slightly calmer voice.

After a brief silence, the men decided to get moving. Three maids arrived with three cleaning carts within minutes. Richard received first aid for his wounds, and the bloody monogrammed towels and broken glass were swept up and bagged. The maids emptied bottles of wine, champagne, and liquor into the cleaning carts, and before long, two men arrived with a piece of table glass that slipped right into the metal frame of the table.

Very few words, if any, were spoken between Mr. Chang and Richard, but they seemed to know what the other was thinking – a common purpose of sorts.

After everything I had put them through, they even shared a few laughs during the mad scramble to fix my handy work. None of it made sense to me. Why would these two men help each other?

By 9:45 a.m. Mr. Chang was fully dressed and back at his post behind the concierge desk. The Presidential suite had been transformed back to its original condition, and the hotel staff that helped nearly destroy it were each given $200 to keep quiet.

"Shall we head home?" asked Richard. "I could use a nap."

"If only it were that simple, easy, and convenient," I thought to myself.

The misery and despair were just beginning for Richard and the entire Bay Area. Powerful forces, most of which were not my doing, had already been put into play the past few days, and all of them were about to collide, causing unimaginable death, destruction, and human despair.

CHAPTER TWELVE

6666666666666666666666666666666666

A Million-dollar Swing

Three days ago, Keyshawn Kidlat hit his second home run of the game. His coach said he could see the stitching right out of the pitcher's hand, which allowed him to predict the ball's movement before it crossed the plate.

"Pitchers make mistakes, and Keesh seems to always take advantage of them," Coach LaDresh told the high school paper. "That boy has a million-dollar swing."

The coach was right. At 17, Keyshawn already had multiple offers to play baseball for dozens of Division I Universities. The professional scouts were also following his senior year at Sacred Heart Cathedral Preparatory.

"The good Lord has given my boy many gifts," Keyshawn's mother would say. "My boy is smart too," she added.

And he was - maintaining a 4.0 GPA going into his final semester of high school as an honor roll student and the last season of his high school baseball career.

"He is by far the most talented kid to come out of our program in decades," coach LaDresh explained. "He also puts butts in the seats, which is a plus for all the players."

Three days ago, Keyshawn walked to the bus stop after putting two over the fence against cross-town archrival Saint Ignatius College Preparatory. He was in good spirits, laughing and joking with some of his teammates along the way. As they called him, *Keesh* would always carry his "lucky bat" wherever he was going. He took practice swings in slow motion at each stoplight and the bus stop while waiting for the MUNI bus that delivered him home each day to his mother. Like most kids, he carried all his textbooks in his backpack and liked to wear a hoodie, proudly displaying the Fighting Irish's green and white.

"I'll catch you later, Keesh; this is my ride," his teammate said. "Ok, James, good game, man."

The bus was late, so Keyshawn put in his music plugs, pulled his hoodie over his head, and continued to swing his lucky bat in slow motion while humming the tunes to his favorite songs. Because of the music, he did not hear the gunshot ring out around the corner from the bus stop. He did not notice the police sirens or the subsequent gunshots, either. He was in the zone, again.

"*Shots fired, shots fired, officer down, I repeat, officer down,*" was broadcast over every police radio. "*Confirm your location, please,*" dispatch replied. "*I have a till tap on the corner of Hayes and Gough, ah, one civilian shot, possible 10-54, one officer down, needs immediate assistance,*" officer Michaels responded. "*Suspect traveling on foot, black male, early twenties, wearing a green hoodie, and backpack. Suspect is armed and dangerous!*"

"*All units, all units, officer needs immediate assistance, the suspect is black male, early 20s, wearing green hoodie and backpack, last seen on foot traveling northbound on Gough Street. The suspect is armed and considered dangerous.*"

After the news hit the police channel, the city erupted with loud sirens reverberating off buildings as every active-duty police officer in the vicinity hit their rollers in heuristic support of their brothers in arms. The information given to them about the suspect being armed and dangerous without gathering all the relevant facts was enough for the cops to make quick, uninformed decisions. The fact that one of their own was shot, possibly dead, made the situation even more brittle. Unfortunately, the dispatched information about an armed young black male wearing a green hoodie and backpack was a salient cue for the decisions that followed.

Keyshawn was still in the zone when officer Michaels approached him on foot. He was mentally going through his at-bats that resulted in strikeouts. In his mind, he looked for an unconscious action that would betray the pitcher and reveal his attempted deception.

"Show me your fastball, Tommy," he said to himself.

He got a changeup and missed. If you can hit the pitch three times out of ten, you will probably earn an excellent living playing professional baseball. Keyshawn was averaging 5 out of 10.

"Possible suspect located at the corner of Eddy and Gough," officer Michaels announced. "I have a young black male, wearing a green hoodie and backpack."

By then, Keyshawn slid his lucky bat into the backpack netting and placed his right hand in his pant pocket. His bus was just one block away.

"Show me your hands," officer Michaels demanded. "Show me your goddamn hands!" he repeated with his handgun drawn and pointed directly at Keyshawn.

Keyshawn finally removed his music plugs and stepped back in immediate terror.

"Show me your hands," officer Michaels demanded again.

"Please, officer, it's nothing; I am just a kid," Keyshawn tried to explain.

"Then show me your hands, boy," officer Michaels demanded.

By then, two patrol cars had arrived at the scene, blocking the intersection. Four police officers were now pointing their weapons at Keyshawn. One of them, a rookie, was aiming the AR-15 found in the patrol car's trunk. All of them were still operating on the information conveyed over the radio – *armed and dangerous*. They did not know that Keyshawn carried it at all times. He liked to rub it for good luck. His mother said it would protect him and help him make good decisions. "Life is too precious to be walking around without his protection and love," she said. "You keep him by your side."

Heuristics are cognitive shortcuts that allow police to make quick decisions without gathering all the essential facts. For instance, had they known Sacred Heart was playing Saint Ignatius for the league championship that evening, then they could have anticipated some young black males wearing green hoodies in the vicinity. Sacred Hearts' school colors were green and white. The fact that Keyshawn's hoody had "Irish" sewn in white cursive across the front of his light green hoodie and the armed robber's hoodie was dark green with no writing would also have been helpful before making any quick decisions. The shootout was two blocks from the high school, and many, if not all, students wore backpacks. The police did not have any of the salient facts. All they knew and were subsequently operating under was that the young black male who allegedly shot one of their own was wearing a green hoodie and backpack.

Keyshawn pulled his right hand from his pocket and said, "please don't shoot."

The rookie officer, whose heart rate was skyrocketing, noticed it in his hand first and yelled out, "GUN!"

Given the officer's cognitive shortcuts, they instinctively decided to unleash hell, firing over 48 rounds of lead bullets into Keyshawn Kidlat's live heart, catapulting him through the shattered glass of the MUNI bus stop and 30 feet down the street. The force of the firepower disintegrated his black chest and badly mutilated his perfect beautiful face.

The boy with the million-dollar swing laid silent, struggling to breathe through his butchered and bloody mouth. The holes in his heart and leaking lungs were gushing blood with every fading beat, and his spine was shattered, riddled with bullet holes. Ravaged by the gunfire, he lay paralyzed, barely speaking through the blood bubbling out of his mouth and chest.

"Ma, ma, mamma," he mumbled.

In his hand was the wooden crucifix his mother had given him. His best friend and teammate, Jackson Barnes, happened to be nearby and ran to him.

"Keesh, it's Jax… come on, buddy…are you there? Stay with me?"

"Ja, Ja...Mamma, ma," Keyshawn mumbled out of his blood-curdling mouth.

Jackson was his sure-handed third baseman and good high school friend. However, he was 17 and still a boy, so he didn't know what to say or do.

"What's happening, Keesh? Come on, man, we have practice tomorrow," Jackson said during the chaos and confusion. "Keyshawn!" Jax then screamed, holding the teams' best player in his lap. But it was way too late and ultimately life-changing for Jackson Barnes as well. A cop immediately ripped Jackson off and away from his friend, then applied his heavy knee to the back of his brittle neck. Jackson was a talented and particularly handsome kid with asthma. After one minute of the heuristic clamp, Jackson quickly lost consciousness, stopped breathing air, suffocated, then nearly died some ten feet from Keyshawn.

Keyshawn Kidlat, the boy with the million-dollar swing, never let go of the wooden crucifix his mother gave him for protection against evil. He died on the city street, lying in a pool of his blood. Jackson Barnes was given a lifesaving mouth-to-mouth resuscitation and slowly regained consciousness.

The Irish would never win the league championship again.

CHAPTER THIRTEEN

6666666666666666666666666666666666

THUNDERSTRUCK

Two days ago, Furland Monroe, Dickie Smits, and Earl James went camping on Mount Diablo. They were life-longfriends, but I considered them to be nothing more than simple dumbshits, so they needed no touch whatsoever.

Rising nearly 4,000 feet above sea level, Mount Diablo is also one of many portals angels use when visiting Earth. Last used in 1906 and again in 1989, the portal's proximity to San Francisco and humanity made it the logical choice.

"Tell me, Furland, your sister still dating that Mexican boy?" asked Dickie.

"She ain't dating him, Dickie, over my dead body," Furland argued. "He just helps with the chores and tends to the chickens, like you."

"That's not what I heard," added Earl. "I heard they come up here for picnics and stuff."

"You ain't heard shit, Earl; now pass me a beer and get the grill going," Furland demanded.

The boys liked to drive up the South Gate road and get drunk at the Live Oak campground once a month or whenever they could. They would bring a small portable gas barbeque because open fire pits were illegal and dangerous due to the dry conditions and seasonal Diablo Winds.

"Did you bring the whiskey?" Furland asked Earl.

"Does your sister date Mexicans? Hell yes, I brought the whiskey," received a group outburst of laughter, even from Furland. "You're such an asshole, Earl, now pass me the bottle."

The men unfolded their camping chairs and began their monthly ritual of chugging cans of cold beer and gulping whiskey or tequila or whatever brown stuff they could put their hands on.

"Check the steaks, Earl, don't burn 'em," Furland demanded.

"I ain't gonna burn the goddamn steaks, Furl," Earl replied, then spit a mouthful of chew on the ground. "Pass it over."

There was a pecking order between the men. Furland was the oldest and had the coolest truck. His family owned a large cattle ranch in the central valley of California. On the other hand, Earl was the biggest and strongest but lacked any real smarts other than grilling meat, fixing old cars, and lighting his farts. Earl worked for Furland's father and, necessarily, Furland. Dickie was scrawny and covered with tattoos. He also worked for the Monroes and had a hidden crush on Furland's sister, Becky, but was too sheepish to do anything about it.

"Who you bringing to the company picnic on Sunday?" Dickie asked Earl.

"Shit, I don't know, Suzie maybe, she seemed answerable to the idea," he replied.

"Answerable? What the hell does that mean?" Dickie asked.

"I think the word you're looking for is amenable, Earl; meaning agreeable, responsive in a cooperative manner," Furland interjected. "Kinda like ready, willing, and able, and the good Lord knows one-eyed Suzie is able," he finished with a smirk.

"Shut up, Furland, she ain't like that no more," Earl responded in defense of his girl.

"What about you, Dickie? You gonna finally nut up and ask Rebecca Monroe to the picnic?" Earl asked, deflecting the conversation about one-eyed Suzie and her recent past prurient requests from her many male suitors.

"Christ, Dickie, why don't you set your sights on someone more amenable to your station in life?" he then asked, highlighting the use of his new word.

"I still don't think you know how to use that word, Earl," Furland once again interjected.

Dickie slugged a mouthful of whiskey, nervously pushing his right knee up and down with the ball of his foot. Once again, he lacked the confidence to respond when it came to his love for Rebecca Monroe. After one more slug, and with the help of the liquid courage, Dickie finally made some progress.

"Maybe I will," was the best he could do.

"What do you think, Furl, y'all think Becky is with that Mexican fella?" Dickie then asked.

"I said she wasn't, goddamnit!" Furland barked.

"But even if she was, my sister sure as shit ain't going with you Dickie. My baby sister is off-limits to you morons."

After a brief uncomfortable silence, Earl raised his cold can of beer and said, "here's to one-eyed Suzie, and that beautiful bullseye on her face," then ripped a loud fart and burped just as he finished his toast. With the perfect timing of the loud fart and belch, all three men burst into almost crying laughter, with Furland spitting out his beer and Earl slowly falling sideways off his chair. In a matter of minutes, they soon forgot about the company picnic, one-eyed Suzie, Rebecca Monroe, or the Mexican boy she was dating. That's how most men are.

After dinner, the boys passed more whiskey around, occasionally relieving themselves in the woods. By then night had fallen, and the warm Diablo winds were periodically blowing through camp. The feel of the warm air made me think of Nero, and the night we burned Rome. But those were very different times, and these were clearly different men. They were honest, straightforward, and lacked absolute conviction. However, what they lacked in sophistication was made even with loyalty and predictability - Earl being the most predictable.

Like clockwork, Earl slowly crept back to camp with his pants halfway down his legs. He always came equipped with a lighter when stalking his prey. The warm air and whiskey were lulling Dickie to sleep, and like any successful predator, Earl sensed his weakness. As he slowly crept toward Dickie, his pants had arrived down around his ankles, restricting his movement. With his pants on the ground, it was most precarious, as Earl's prey could hear the drag of his trousers or the scraping of his boots along the warm sandstone and alert him to the danger. Tonight, however, Dickie was unaware of the impending attack due to his semi-inebriated condition. Earl was in the perfect position to strike. He turned around and bent over, then reached back and lit the torch.

"How about we get rid of that ear hair, Dickie?"

Earl's fart immediately ignited, sending a gaseous stream of fire out of his asshole, engulfing Dickie's right ear and face. Dickie, jerked out of his peaceful slumber by the flames, leaped to his feet, spilling the bottle of whiskey on his lap. He was stunned, so Earl initiated another attack.

"Let's dry you off, brother," he said while backing up toward Dickie. "You look like you could use another."

The second burst of flames flew out of his ass, hitting Dickie in the chest, igniting the spilled whiskey for a brief second. Then, in a panic, Dickie jumped up and down, frantically brushing his shirt and rubbing his head at the same time. Furland and Earl were locked in painful laughter as they watched him jump and squeal and shout.

"Goddamn you, Earl; you son of bitch, I'm gonna get you," Dickie screamed after finishing up his fart flame dance.

After Dickie regained his composure, with all the excitement over, the three men settled back down to drinking, spitting, telling stories and lies. Earl was very content, knowing he had pulled off another successful attack. Dickie was oddly happy because even though he was the usual target of Earl's fart flames, he felt a sense of belonging to a loyal and select group of friends. And Furland sat back with a content smile and sense of pride, happy to oversee his simple gang of three unwavering friends for life. The night had been perfect.

The men eventually began drifting off to sleep. Like everything else between them, their sleeping arrangements were set by custom, tradition, and routine. Furland always slipped away first, sleeping under a wool blanket in the back seat of his truck. Earl and Dickie liked to stay up a bit later, talking about girls and fishing. However, like clockwork, Earl would make his way to the bed of Furland's truck and fall asleep on an old foam pad. Dickie would smoke all of his cigarettes and stare up at the stars until he finished the bottle. He routinely would wake up during the coldest part of the night and crawl into the truck bed next to Earl and shiver himself to sleep. Their routines filled up the dry summer and fall months for years. Furland, Dickie, and Earl were kings on those occasions and probably heading toward Diablo folklore. But, unfortunately, mother nature can be contrary and ruin tradition.

A shaft of precipitation was falling just over their heads that night, completely evaporating as it fell through the lower dry layers of the atmosphere. Such storms occur during the summer months, especially over Mount Diablo. Tonight, as the rain fell and evaporated, the clouds held another powerful and destructive surprise.

The first lightning strike hit the ground with such force it arced through the old oak tree Furland parked his truck under, causing one of the heavier limbs to explode and catch fire simultaneously. The air beneath the storm had been cooling from the falling rain, causing it to descend and rapidly fan out upon impacting the ground. The fire started by the lightning strike was easily fanned by the storm winds, pushing the flames to spread rapidly. The dry soil and sand were immediately picked up by the strong winds, creating a dust devil. With so much dry fuel and gusty wind, the fire spread quickly.

It wasn't until the second bolt of lightning struck and the roar of thunder rattled the atmosphere that the men woke up from their drunken stupor. By then, it was too late. The campground was quickly engulfed in flames burning up every tree and bush. The storm winds acted like a wand, directing the fire in every direction. Eventually, the oak tree that had stood through time came crashing down onto Furland's truck, crushing Earl and Dickie to a slow and miserable death.

Furland managed to crawl from his truck and get to his feet just in time for the oxygen to be sucked from his lungs as the firestorm roared back through camp, incinerating Furland and every living thing in its path.

Two days ago, Furland Monroe, Dickie Smits, and Earl James started out their day as kings; then got consumed by flames and passed into ashen folklore.

CHAPTER FOURTEEN

6666666666666666666666666666666666666

HANDS UP, DON'T SHOOT

Today, Keyshawn Kidlat would be laid to rest by his parents, extended family, teammates, students, teachers, politicians, the Mayor of San Francisco, and hundreds of television reporters with cameras. His tragic death and shooting by the SFPD sparked a national outrage. Burying Sacred Hearts' golden boy had ignited a divided nation.

Images of the shooting were captured by dozens of kids and onlookers, landing the gruesome footage on the 6 o'clock news for two days after his death. The police were anticipating widespread protests and the possibility of riots and looting. Although, I admit things were looking up for me because I love it when humans get unhinged.

In one corner were the *Justice for Keyshawn* folks, very organized and highly motivated by his mother, Gloria Kidlat, a nurse from the hood you call Hunter's Point. On the other hand, there was a riotous group of social outcasts, common criminals, and deadbeat thugs whose only objective was to apply their ignorance, desperation, and thievery upon human society. And in the middle were the outnumbered cops.

My friend, Titus, would have erased the riotous group of common criminals from your Earth, killing every one of them where they stood. Back then, I truly wished he was present when the Vandal hordes ransacked Cortina. If so, maybe

Avelina would have lived longer or maybe given her wings back. Nonetheless, given their skill for weapon-smithing and war-horsing, my bitter two-thousand-year-old grudge against the Vandals has remarkably turned into mild admiration for their conviction of purpose and cold-hearted brutality.

All the same, the Justice for Keyshawn movement sparked national outrage, as I said, over police brutality, social injustice, and systemic inequality amongst the races. However, I honestly don't understand what they were complaining about because this sort of thing has been going on since I arrived here on Earth. Marcus Aurelius was right - nothing new at all, as far as I could decipher.

"Y'all gonna stand up straight and make sure Keyshawn didn't die for nothing," Gloria instructed the crowd of 500 or so marchers through her loudspeaker. The group gathered around her at the bottom of Market Street in Justin Herman Plaza as the human sense of loss started to rumble.

"We are never going back to that Jim Crow bullshit," she shouted. "Nothing gonna change that," she angrily preached.

· · · · · · · · · ·

I remember a group of white men I touched back in 1865 who were from Pulaski, Tennessee. They were returning from another human war. They formed a private club for confederate veterans, which grew into a secret society terrorizing black communities. Before that, I enjoyed the last vestiges of Roman culture - slavery.

"Here, put this on your head," I told him in jest.

"My brother is dead, sir, no less because of that slave-loving president, Lincoln," John informed me.

In 1865, I touched John Wilkes Booth. He was almost no different than Richard Daily at that time, just looking for a job, I assumed. But then, BOOM, to the back of Lincoln's head, John surprised me, giving me remembrances of my winemaker friend Baptiste. Johnny had killed your president, but I didn't get to see the life draining out of Abraham's dying eye. Unfortunately, Johnny deprived me of that by his selfish nature.

Soon after, Johnny's friends started wearing silly white hoods over their heads when creeping through white Southern society. With Lincoln gone, they took to a character performed by a playwright I had touched, Thomas Dartmouth Rice.

"Daddy Rice," as he was known professionally, used to chalk his face and hands with burnt Portuguese corkwood, dress up in ragged clothes, torn shoes, and a tattered gentleman's hat, and impersonate a witty dark-skinned slave field hand. He called this irreverent character - Jim Crow.

"Come listen, boyz and gulls, I'za gonna sing y'all a good ole fashion nigger work song," Jim Crow would say while jumping up and down, slapping his ass on stage.

The whites got a real kick out of his foolish and generally harmful depiction of African Americans. Sometime later, the boys who hid behind their white sheets started naming their many segregation laws after Mr. Rice's demeaning character. I guess they figured by separating the whites from the blacks would preserve their decent white society.

"Lord has mercy, even with you, Beez," Daddy Rice told me before taking the stage. So, I humored the old fool.

"Are blacks better than whites?" I asked Daddy Rice.

"Bite your tongue, boy," he replied. "The Lord made us the superior race," he abruptly responded, crediting my father with such falsehoods.

"Is that why you like to enslave the blacks?" I asked.

"Son, that's what they were born to be, under God's eye, of course," he replied while chalking his face black.

"So, humans are not all the same?" I continued, only to confuse him with my silly questions.

"In God's eyes, no sir, they most certainly are not," he replied.

Of course, he was mistaken.

Despite the many different color shades he gave humans, my father didn't see them as inferior or superior. Instead, he just kept adding pieces to the puzzle when things didn't fit, then created newer pieces for his pleasure when he got bored.

He thought of everything. Making some humans strong and fast, or just strong, or just fast. He made some with blue eyes and others with brown eyes. He made some who could sing, and some who could make music, and some who could do both. He made some that were logical and some that were more free-spirited. God even made some that were open to new ideas, which gave them the power of thought, like my friend Aristotle teaches. But the worst were the ones he made ignorant, believing my father had a plan. We called them idiots. They have always been around, the idiots, ever since Jesus roamed the Earth.

Back then, Jez, as I called him, was given a pass. He liked to play with the idiots, making them believe there was a power from above that could fix your life. Devotion to him would solve the human question – why do I exist?

Jez was nice enough, and I think he had fun with humanity well before I arrived. So did my father. He often roiled the masses for "shits and giggles." However, I believe he prefered to play with humans, like chest pieces. I guess they both liked to play with the idiots. They loved idiots. The problem with the idiots, of course, was their sheer number— so many idiots.

Ultimately, in my opinion, my father created anything he could come up with or mold.

Red hair, blond hair, black hair. Tall, short, fat, skinny. It didn't matter to God because they were all his creatures. The problems only started happening when some clever humans took free will too far.

"Beez, father gave us idiots to play with, but have mercy on them, for they do not know," my older brother once told me at school when I was young.

"What don't they know?" I asked Dagon.

"Who they are or what their purpose is," he said to me rather matter of factly. The bell rang, and Dagon ran off. But I never forgot that day. I also never understood what he was saying.

Maybe Dagon decided he was tired of the game and took them off his board. Or maybe, our father told him he was supposed to bring hope to the idiots. I don't know. I am confident, however, that neither Jez, Dagon, or my father concocted human slavery or war amongst humans. That was all you.

Gloria Kidlat was facing the same difficulties that had occurred back in 1870 to black folks.

"My boy's death will not be in vain so help me, God," she promised.

Gloria Kidlat had a voice. She sang for her church choir and spoke three different languages. She was beautiful and eloquent, unlike her husband Reginald "Reggie" Kidlat. Reggie was quiet and led from behind. I liked him, notwithstanding his other gruff character traits.

I watched them both during my time with the Zodiac. Gloria graduated from that incendiary institution in Berkeley that taught their students to believe in and fight for social justice and equal rights for all human beings. The University equipped her with mental acuity, reason, logic, and the silly belief that intelligent humans could change society.

I've seen it time and time again. Eventually, men like Nero, Hitler, or Stalin come along and try to exterminate the elitist shits so that they can rule the ignorant masses. It works for a while on the idiots until the subsequent uprising of intellectuals finds an army to put them down. America did that in 1942. Even still, in my experience, evil pursuits tend to spring up and recycle every 20 years or so. It only takes one man. Nevertheless, I see potential in the current leader of the free world.

I also know about the general principles of Greek law. Before my fall, I spent time with Alexander the Great during his lessons with Aristotle. Aristotle believed that certain customs of settling a difference between two states, or humans, should be accomplished through external arbitration and, of course, logic. Commerce or inheritance aside, the Greeks devised a system where humans could resolve their differences – and it worked for many hundreds of years. But not today. Not now. There was too much anger brewing.

"Hands up, don't shoot," Gloria began to chant.

"Hands up, don't shoot," the angry masses replied.

"What do we want?" she then added.

"Justice!"

"When do we want it?"

"Now!"

"Hands up, don't shoot," "Hands up, don't shoot...."

The organized mob then set out, slowly moving and jolting, as a rowdy bunch. The *Justice for Keyshawn* people marched down Market Street toward City Hall. Their path would take them past the Four Seasons Hotel, me and Richard, then into a wall of riot police mounted on horses.

Again, horses.

CHAPTER FIFTEEN

66666666666666666666666666666666666

FIRESTORM

Furland, Dickie, and Earl's deaths went largely unnoticed the day after the lightning bolts started what firefighters were calling the Live Oak Fire. The Diablo winds were pushing the flames down the hillside and west toward the town of Danville. With the fire burning so hot and the winds pushing the fire to eat, nothing was safe in its path

Bob and Judy Spatchcock lived in Danville, a very affluent and pleasant town that sits on the southern base of Mount Diablo. The Spatchcocks were in their late eighties and managed to get around ok. Bob mostly raised his only daughter, Delores, in that home. The Spatchcocks resided there for the better part of 50 years. Delores's parents had seen fires break out on Mount Diablo's slopes before, but each time the fire crews would extinguish the flames before they became a concern.

"Mom, you guys ok?" Delores asked her mother over the phone. "The news I'm getting says you need to evacuate."

"We will be fine, DD. They always put out the fires before they reach us," Judy replied. "How's Tom? Are you still seeing that boy?" she asked.

"No, yes, I don't know, mom, things are complicated right now, but listen to me, you and dad need to pack a bag and get somewhere safe," Delores begged her mother.

"Your father wants to talk to you; hold on," Judy demurred. "Sweetie, it's DD; come talk to her, please dear," she hollered away from the phone.

Mothers and daughters are different from fathers and sons. Judy had endured years of her uppity, smarter than history, kind of daughter. Old age and time just wore out the natural motherly affection she once had for her daughter. So, Judy stopped trying years ago.

"Wait mom, please listen to…."

"How's my big shot attorney doing today?" her father then jumped in mid-sentence.

"Daddy, dad, you need to listen to me; that fire is burning out of control and heading your way; you packed a bag, right?" Delores asked.

"I'm keeping an eye on it, pumpkin, don't worry, I've got the hoses out and keeping things wet," her father foolishly responded, without fully appreciating the seriousness of the looming threat.

"Tell her we are coming to town next week for your birthday," Judy said while handing Bob his blood pressure pills.

"How's work? Are they keeping you busy, dear?" Bob said at the same time.

"Yes, dad, I'm busy, but you are not listening to me," Delores said with a raised voice. "The fire is burning out of control, and you need to evacuate!" she repeated herself in a more forceful tone.

"Tell her we have reservations at the North Beach Café," Judy yelled out from the other room.

"Your mother says we have reservations, I guess," Bob added. "Where?" he then shouted back at his wife.

"I just told you, Robert," Judy said in her complaining voice.

"What?" Bob replied in his irritated voice.

"The police are here, Bob; can you call her back?" Judy hollered back while tucking herself into an afternoon tv talk show.

"What?" Bob shouted again.

I suppose the concept of *home* is the one thing in common we angels have with humans. A place to safely return to provides comfort and relaxation to everybody. The need for some dirt to defend and call our own is in all of us. To weather the storm or feel safe at night is universally necessary amongst both humans and angels. But the one thing my father never planned for was a fire. Your homes would simply never endure that threat. You still try, nonetheless. For humans, the need to call a place "home" began with caves and primitive huts, then developed over time to castles, estates, mansions, ranches, and even simple, comfortable homes like the Spatchcocks.

Bob built his home in 1964. It was spacious and modest. Together with his father, he constructed many homes throughout the '60s, '70s, and 1980s. *Spatchcock Family Builders* developed most of the cities of Danville, Dublin, and Livermore. Mr. Spatchcock died in 1977 and left everything to his only son. Bob retired back in 1997 a wealthy man. Delores would get it all.

"Honey, your mother and I have lived in this old house for over 50 years," Bob told his only daughter. "I've seen that mountain catch fire before, and we have always survived," he promised her.

"Dad, fires are different now," Delores tried to explain.

"Honey, I can't just pack up your mother and leave. Our entire life is here – yours too. Now stop worrying, we will be fine," Bob assured his daughter.

"Will you go see what they want," Judy then yelled from her sofa.

"Who?" Bob asked.

"We're fine, hold on," Bob said to his daughter. "Pumpkin, the house is starting to growl, and I think someone is at the front door. Can I call you back?"

Bob had poor hearing, especially when he didn't wear his aid. He said the aids irritated his large hairy ears, but I tend to believe he liked to have an excuse for not hearing his nagging wife's frequent questions and redundant daily orders.

"Dad...dad?" Delores spoke.

"We're fine, hold on," Bob said.

Ordinarily, Bob would probably be correct, and he and his wife would be fine. Historically, the fire crews would contain and douse the flames before reaching his house. But that was before, and this is now. The relative humidity was rapidly dropping in the Diablo Valley, sucking moisture from the trees and every other living organism. Especially the houses and the oaks. Even Bob's sturdy beams and posts started to dry up and splinter.

"What's that noise?" Judy asked her husband before falling asleep.

Bob didn't know, but every stitch of life and living organism on the mountain was getting consumed by fire. The flames, however, still appeared to be terrorizing the mountain at a relatively safe distance from Bob's front lawn.

"Sir, we're asking every resident to evacuate," rookie officer Dean Smith said.

"Son, go check on the others; we will be fine," Bob told the young officer.

"Mr. Spatchcock, this thing is coming fast, and you're at the end of the block, sir. The only way out is one way," officer Smith insisted. "If the fire jumps 680, you will be trapped."

"We'll be fine, son, Go check on the Johnsons, and we will be right behind you," Bob promised.

"Sir, the winds are picking up, I'll be back in 5 minutes. It would be best if you were ready to go when I return," officer Smith replied.

"We will be gone well before then, Dean, so don't bother coming back," Bob promised.

"Thank you, Mr. Spatchcock. I'll hold you to your word."

Set in his ways, Bob didn't mean what he said. Routine and old age made him disregard the looming threat. That's the thing about the Diablo winds; you never know when they may kick up into a fit. As Bob stood on his front porch, within minutes after officer Smith sped away, ash, embers, smoke, and flames were suddenly being pushed by new gusts of wind, reaching 80 and 90 miles per hour. With so much oxygen, the fire grew hotter and more ferocious by the minute. Before Bob could turn on his garden hose, the flames jumped the six-lane freeway and began to set fire to the homes down the street. Old oak trees that stood for hundreds of years became instantly engulfed by fire, and the sky turned black except for the glowing red ball overhead that was the Sun. His house kept cricking and cracking as the fire pulled the remaining moisture from the old home.

Cars started to catch fire and explode or just melt. It was all happening so fast that Bob barely managed to turn the faucet on before a sick, empty feeling overwhelmed his ability to act. Finally, when his neighbor's house caught fire, reality set in at the futility of his actions, so he dropped the useless garden hose and ran inside to find Judy asleep on their couch.

"Judy, honey, wake up, baby, we have to go now," Bob pleaded with his wife while patting her on the face.

"What's that smell? What's going on?" she replied, half asleep.

"The fire jumped the freeway; we need to go," he explained to his groggy wife. "No time to think, just get up and come with me," he said with a shortened breath.

When Bob and Judy reemerged from their home, the entire block was ablaze. Smaller fires were now starting to ignite on their roof and lawn. Bob rushed his wife to their old red Mercedes Benz 450 SL convertible, opened the passenger-side door, and helped Judy into the tattered leather seat. He then trotted around the front of the car and hopped in the driver's seat as the roof of his old house was now completely ablaze. There was nothing he could do but start the car and flee.

"Hold on to your hat, dear. This is gonna get pretty sporty," he said to his wife in a surprisingly calm voice.

Bob then chirped his tires and threw his red car into reverse, catapulting the old rig onto Lake Street. Just then, a sea of bright orange embers blew across the surface of the street, where Delores and the other neighborhood kids used to play. The air was so hot that it burned their throats with every gasp of precious oxygen. The fire was eating up the arid countryside by then, sending plumes of black smoke into the darkening skies across the Bay Area and beyond. The flames were so hot that motors melted right out of hastily abandoned cars, and the molten liquid drained down the owner's driveway. Eventually, the fire would reduce all the trees on Bob's once-lush street to blackened skeletal remains or piles of glowing ash.

"We're gonna make it, honey, just hold on," Bob assured his wife. "Just need to get to the end of the street."

Bob flew across the sea of ash and embers, taking his sturdy old Benz up to 90 mph. He thought to himself; *this isn't my time,* and so went faster and closer to the safety of the next intersection and away from his burning cul-de-sac.

"Once we get through the light and onto the main street, we should be fine," he promised his terrified wife.

"Slow down, Bob, for God's sake, you're going to get us killed," Judy complained while digging in her purse for her summer scarf.

But Bob was focused on the road ahead.

He also didn't hear a word she said. With both sides of the road burning with flames dancing up trees some four stories high, he set his narrow focus on the end of the road. His tunnel vision and deafness gave him the necessary will to speed. Unfortunately, it also blinded him from the old stop sign at Spring Street. With winds now gusting up to nearly 100 mph and flames doing the jive in every direction, he just maintained his laser focus on the stoplight two football fields ahead and floored the pedal with an innate will to survive.

So was Officer Smith. He was rolling hot with the Johnsons in the back of his patrol car down Spring Street. Officer Smith had the sirens howling and the cherry lights spinning in unison when he entered the intersection at breakneck speed. He believed the neighborhood was evacuated, as promised, and was understandably panicked given the unstoppable death and destruction the firestorm was inflicting on the area. Bob never heard the siren or saw the rollers. He just held Judy's hand.

"Hold on, dear, almost there."

Bob and Dean were immune from each other up until that last split second.

Officer Smith's patrol car struck Bob's red Benz's passenger side door with such force it nearly sliced the car in half. Judy, who forgot to secure her seatbelt, was instantly thrown from the convertible about 100 feet before bouncing off the distant neighbor's front door and coming to rest in the burning juniper bushes that lined their front yard. She would remain there until the fire transformed her lifeless body into a pile of cremated bone bits and gray, ashen powder.

Officer Smith's cruiser ricocheted off Bob's sturdy Benz and came to rest several hundred feet down Lake Street. The old Mercedes was left lifeless on her side, leaking oil, fluid, and gas. Bob remained strapped in tight with his femur bone snapped in half and protruding out of his pants.

The shock of it all, and I suspect every ounce of his adrenaline, kept Bob's attention on unbuckling and crawling away from the mangled wreck. He managed to crawl 20 feet before recognizing the splintered thigh bone poking through his bloody trousers. Hot embers were blowing into his face and mouth and eyes with every excruciatingly painful attempt to drag his body away from the smoldering wreck. The hair on his arms curled from the heat, and the ember balls burned small patches from his eyebrows. Eventually, the Mercedes caught fire and was engulfed in flames within seconds – then exploded.

"Mr. Spatchcock, sir, you've been in a bad accident," Officer Smith habitually spoke the obvious while attempting to pick up Bob from under his armpits. His head had suffered a nasty laceration and was pumping a lot of blood down his face. Unfortunately, he was unaware of the compound fracture Bob had endured.

"AAAAH, put me down, my leg, my leg," Bob screamed in agony as more flaming embers peppered his face with stinging pain.

"I'm sorry, sir, but we have to get you some help," Officer Smith said while ignoring Bob's screams of agony. "Hang on, sir, just a few more yards," he promised while dragging him away from the wreck.

"Judy, where is Judy?" Bob cried out.

"Who, sir?"

"My wife, where is she?"

Officer Smith then noticed the critical bone protruding from Bob's thigh. So, he reactively dropped him and looked the other way.

"I need your belt, now," Officer Smith screamed while watching the torrid flames encircle them. "I need to put a tourniquet on that, sir, before we go any further," he tried to explain. By cinching his upper thigh with the belt, it would help stop the increasing blood flow leaking from his body and possibly save Mr. Spatchcock's life.

"Take long slow breaths if you can, sir. You might start to feel some nausea and fatigue," Officer Smith informed him.

With the world around him going up in flames, Officer Smith kept to his wits, even after glancing at Judy's burning corpse smoldering under low flames on Bob's neighbor's juniper bushes.

"Get up, sir, trust me," he told Bob while making up his mind. "We have no time left," he said with urgency.

But Bob was sweating profusely and starting to lose consciousness. His dead weight made it even more challenging to move.

"It's time to go," Officer Smith barked again while pulling Bob's thigh belt tight.

"Awww," he screamed in pain.

"Save my wife, please," he mumbled after.

By then, the Johnsons had set out on foot to escape the fire and hopefully find some help. The fire kept burning, of course. The chaos of the moment, however, left the entire town of Danville largely unprepared and dumbfounded. It was what you humans call a mighty clusterfuck of gigantic proportions. But, of course, there was nothing he could say or do that would soften that reality. No amount of candy-coating or white lies could get around the harsh truth.

"Get up, for fuck's sake," Officer Smith shouted.

"Where is she, my wife? Bob begged.

"She is gone, sir. I'm sorry, but she is dead, and we need to go, now," Officer Smith replied, now fearing for his safety.

As it turned out, Judy was right; Bob's driving would get her killed.

Officer Smith then turned the key in the ignition, but his car had finally succumbed to the collision, bleeding out her precious fluids and oils. The cruiser's tires were melting rubber onto the hot cement when he jumped into action.

"Change of plan, sir; we need to make a run for it. Hop on," Officer Smith said while hoisting Bob onto his back.

"Aaaww," Bob groaned from the effort.

"Hold on, sir, we're gonna make it," he promised.

Officer Smith then broke into a slow jog with Bob on his back, chugging his way up the street and through the surrounding fire and dancing flames while getting pelted with bits and pieces of burning hot embers. He carried Bob nearly a mile before stopping to rest. He eventually reached the local high school football field, some three miles from the crash, and slowly fell to his knees in the presence of other survivors, doctors, and nurses.

"His leg is badly broken. You! Help this man, now," he screamed.

Officer Dean Smith then ran back toward the flames. I never understood that. Why would a man sacrifice his life for another? Humans are unique in that regard, I suppose.

"There may be others who need help," he shouted on his way.

It was suicide, in my opinion, but he did it anyway. What I thought to be foolish certainly changed my mind about human beings, especially after what Officer Smith managed. Some innate, loyal devotion to duty or honor or both gave them the willpower to do incredible acts of courage and bravery in the service of their fellow humans.

"There's one more!" a man yelled at Dean, coming from the fires with a dog in his arms.

"You! Sir, come with me," another man ordered.

"What's your name, son?" he asked me.

"My name?" I responded. "It's ah Bee...."

"Nevermind, it's not important, hold this," he then cut me off while handing me a small red fire extinguisher.

"What am I supposed to do with this?" I sincerely thought to myself.

As I looked at the forty-foot killing flames devouring all that was good and normal, it felt like Rome all over again. The heat, burning fire, and resultant destruction made it so. God's animals and lovely people were trapped in a vicious, losing battle. Even the neighbor's rabbits died. Down the road, Sergeant Randy Williston ran into the fire, right behind Officer Dean Smith. The firestorm was winning. It always does, of course. Just large portions of humanity, losing, constantly losing.

Randy went first, burned to a crisp because of his bravery. Dean tried to save him, then he collapsed from exhaustion. His death was just as grotesque. Know this, the smell of burning bodies devourers your soul and stains your heart. It even saddens some angels. In the end, both men were heroes, I suppose, but not really. Not like you would think. They just died horribly and in pain. Heroism is a farce because both men could only leave their ashes behind, nothing more, nothing less, just worthless, stupid ashes. And for what?

Randy and Dean were heroes and fools. Unfortunately, death is just better than heroism. Death always wins.

CHAPTER SIXTEEN

66666666666666666666666666666666

HORSEPLAY

As you know, I'm not too fond of horses, even though they have served humanity well over the years. Horses are handsome and probably brilliant. They are the epitome of elegance and wisdom, according to my father. Moreover, they are physically powerful, generally trusted, and have been blessed by God. Think about it: the Quarter Horse, the world's fastest equine sprinter, has been clocked at 55 mph. Imagine a thousand pounds of muscle and hard-charging bone hitting your head. And yet, despite their superior physical dominance and predisposition for high jinks, I was fortunate enough to discover one method to tame the finicky beasts. Upon his return to Cortina, Titus Septimus shared with me a means to make them suffer. Although they are immune to my touch, horses, as it turns out, have no defense against a lovely microscopic parasite called *Giardia lamblia*.

Although Titus shared my disdain for Vandals, he cast no blame upon the horse for the death of Avelina. He returned in May after her death.

"How dare he raid my domain and kill my plebes," he responded to the news of her death.

"What will you do, Titus?" I asked.

"Well, teacher, this will not go unpunished, I assure you, the Vandal king and his horsemen will suffer," he responded.

"But how will you deal with his Warhorses? They seem invincible," I questioned.

"Give them some beaver fever, then unleash hell," he said with supreme confidence.

"What, may I ask, is beaver fever?" I said.

"Something the legions discovered up north. It's in the water. We think it came from the streams dammed by beavers. Toothy little bastards wreak havoc on the trees," he said.

"What does it do?" I asked. "The beaver fever?"

"It causes severe diarrhea, stomach cramps, nausea, and dehydration, especially amongst the buggering regulars," he informed me. "They get so sick that they are unable to fight," he said with a smile.

Titus informed me how they collected barrels of the contaminated water from the streams damned by beavers and experimented on slaves by giving them the bad water. Within days the slaves who drank the tainted water were struck down with chronic explosive diarrhea, dehydration, and painful, debilitating cramps lasting several weeks. He also explained that even the all-powerful horse was not immune to the effects of the water. But, as it turned out, it wasn't the water but a tiny protozoan organism in the water that infects the small intestines of mammals, including horses.

Titus sent spies into the Vandal camp and polluted their water supply with the tiny parasite four days before his attack. By the fifth day, the entire Vandal tribe was suffering and rendered weak and useless. The big blond, blue-eyed men could barely lift a sword or pull back a bow. Even their unstoppable Warhorses were experiencing diarrhea, hair loss, ill thrift, and weight loss.

As promised, on the fifth day, Titus unleashed hell on the Vandal tribe that took my Avelina from me. In short order, his men burned their entire village to the ground and murdered all the men and boys. He also allowed his soldiers to rape the women. Titus spared the horses because of their value.

"Your hatred of the horse must stop, teacher. It's not their fault," he said.

Nonetheless, he enslaved the remaining children and surviving women and promptly marched his growing army back to Cortina.

I rather enjoyed that day up north. Watching Titus' men rain fire and death upon the Vandals seemed just and fair. But I still couldn't forgive the horses. Since then, I've played with the microscopic timebomb on a few occasions. I once spilled them into the many male bathhouses that used to populate the City of San Francisco back in 1981 – watching with delight as the tubs turned brown.

It's also the one thing I have over horses - the parasite. The beautiful and destructive organism that unconsciously swims in freshwater, with an unknown purpose, instinctively attaching itself to your lower intestines, devoted to eating and festering within humans and, more importantly, the equine's body. Killing or consuming all nutritious passerbys until nothing but liquid shit and brain vexing muscle pain chew you up. My friend, the parasite, is a true and wonderful gift from Titus.

I keep a ready supply of water tainted with *Giardia* at my disposal. In fact, with all the rising social tension mounting in San Francisco, I decided to pay a visit to the SFPD Mounted Patrol Unit in Golden Gate Park the day after the police murdered Keyshawn Kidlat. On most days, the officers on horseback are patrolling Golden Gate Park, Pier 39, Union

Square, and downtown – for show. The officers' height gives them a clear view of crowds, and the horses' incredible size and conspicuous presence serve as a significant crime deterrent. Nonetheless, it occurred to me that there may be a need for crowd control in the days to come. The ever-growing mob of protestors and, necessarily, the opportunistic band of criminals, looters, and vandals that take advantage of social outrage would undoubtedly blend in with the righteous marchers and social activists like Reggie and Gloria Kidlat.

I suspect my microscopic friend was all set, having found his way to the trusty steeds' lower intestine by the time Gloria was leading her hundreds of protestors down Market Street. With the mounted patrol and 50 or so riot police lining up at one end and the growing mob marching in their direction, it would only take one spark to set it off.

Richard and I were walking into a literal shit storm.

CHAPTER SEVENTEEN

6666666666666666666666666666666666

RIOT

As Gloria Kidlat led her organized group of justice blowhards down Market Street toward City Hall, more and more disorganized and chaotic herds of people began spilling into Market Street, much like tributaries flow into rivers. Like those tributaries, the further downstream the mob traveled, the more people filled with resentment, distrust, and anger poured into Market Street's main river of outrage. Like a heavy rainstorm that starts in the mountains and rapidly drains into creeks and rivers, the flash flood of protestors soon became indistinguishable from the opportunistic and lawless hordes of disenfranchised social outcasts, hoods, hooligans, and petty criminals that were filling the streets.

Make no mistake, as is the case with most flash floods, eventually the river bursts its banks, causing catastrophic damage to everything in its unchecked path of destruction. Planned or not, Gloria's 500 organized protestors quickly grew into 5,000 unruly, uncontrolled, and unpredictable rioters.

From high atop his trusty steed *Buster*, mounted patrolman Freddy Egan, Jr. nervously watched as the river of humanity flowed his way.

"Are you seeing this?" Freddy asked his fellow patrolmen over the walkie-talkie.

Merrr, Mer, Buster added.

"What the fuck? What's wrong, Buster?" Freddy asked Buster as he started to fail.

"Captain, we may have a problem, sir, here, ah... there are more than 500," Egan then shouted into his chest-mounted walkie-talkie.

It was great because Buster's ass had just broken loose, spraying a foul-smelling green liquid of putrid shit all over Officer Bill O'Callaghan's riot shield and boots.

"Ah, shit, what the fuck," he said while attempting to wipe the green liquid off his boots.

My lovely parasite had done its job, cooking Buster's intestines after he drank from the tainted trough of horse water. When Richard and I stepped outside of the hotel, all hell was beginning to break loose.

"Sir, there is a fuck load of humanity coming our way," patrolman Egan reaffirmed his nervous concern. "Something is not right with Buster and the horses. We need backup, fast!"

At first, we scampered along the sidewalk, avoiding the growing masses. Richard was still hungover and in bad shape from his fall, so I asked for the backpack and told him to stay close.

"Where on God's green earth are all these people coming from?" Richard said out loud. "They all can't be protestors, can they?" He was still drunk, stoned, and suffering from the trembling after-effects of our debaucherously lovely evening.

As we moved slowly through the crowds, a group of about two dozen black-clad demonstrators quickly gathered ahead of us, holding signs that read: "Crush Fascism" and "Nazis Get Fucked!"

"Who are these guys?" I asked Richard.

"Counter protestors, I suspect. Maybe people who hate the president," he explained.

It suddenly made sense to me because I remember touching him many years ago while playing cards in Atlantic City. He's been rather busy since - doing some evil duty.

Simultaneously, many protestors wearing red "Make America Great Again" hats and carrying American flags were marching up Grant Street. Rumors soon spread on social media that the *Puff boys*, a far-right, neo-fascist, chauvinist, exclusively male organization known for promoting and committing political violence, were among the hundreds of MAGATS ready to brawl. That's what I call them – MAGATS.

Heading right into the center of the fascist puff boys and anti-fascist liberals were throngs of opportunistic vandals, looters, and petty criminals marching alongside Gloria Kidlat's righteous protestors. Their collision was inevitable, and all it needed was a violent and fiery spark.

With tensions rapidly building, Captain Thomas Fairbairn called in the riot police. He ordered 50 officers in protective riot gear to march down O'Farrell Street and seal off its intersection with Grant Street, forcing the MAGATS into Market Street. Simultaneously, another platoon of riot police was assembling on 4th Street where it meets Market Street. Within minutes, the MAGATS, puff boys, black-clad anti-fascist, righteous Justice for Keyshawn protestors, looters, vandals, petty criminals, and the innocent were squeezed into Market Street where Grant and O'Farrell streets connect. A perfect triangle of hate had formed.

There was nowhere for anyone to go with rows of horse-mounted officers, a flying wedge of riot police, and, my favorite, snatch squads blocking all exits. Metaphorically speaking, a critical mass was about to be unleashed on the streets of San

Francisco with no real definitive social change behind it, just pure chaos, madness, violence, and eventual beautiful bloodshed.

As the horses advanced up Market Street, many MAGATS and puff boys slipped behind the line and ended up across the street from the black-clad anti-fascists. As usual, it didn't take much to set it off – just an Orange.

He came from a wealthy family, educated at that landmark of progressive thinking in Berkeley. With all the privilege possible, Billy Anderson could have been anywhere in the world, but he chose to express himself on the streets of San Francisco.

Richard and I were making our way down Market Street in hopes of taking a left on 4th Street and away from the suffocating crowds. As I passed by young Billy, I fell prey to my nature and touched him. I couldn't help myself.

"Hand me an orange," he then said to his roommate. "Go to hell, You Nazi bastards," he screamed.

The orange hit Lloyd "Nutter" Hewitt square in the face, slightly breaking his nose upon impact. The juice from the tasty fruit scattered across his eyes, causing them to water and burn. Nutter's fellow puff boys were displeased by the assault and immediately attacked Billy and his naïve roommate.

"Time to kick some ass, boys," one backward bumpkin hollered. Another just let out a stupid country howl. "Yeehaw!"

Billy was punched in the face and kicked in the balls, dropping him instantly. During Billy's crouch, his roommate was hit over the back of the head with a scaly fish club as he tried to retreat. Several other random anti-fascists then came to their defense, also wielding fists and clubs and knives.

By the time Nutter came to his senses and joined the melee, he was punched in the nose by an anti-fascist, completely breaking it, opening a faucet of blood down his chest. The color red seems to excite humans, especially men. Groups of three and four from one side of the brawl immediately ganged up on one or two from the other. The melee devoured Billy and Chance. Their blood quickly painted the streets.

Richard was just about to make a left onto 4th Street and away from the brawl when the newly formed riot squad came rushing forward in a flying wedge formation with shields and wood batons. They were determined to break through the bloody confrontation and force the unhinged crowd of MAGATS, puff boys, looters, black-clad anti-fascist, Billy, and Chance up Market Street.

Further ahead, more of the horses had succumbed to the potent parasite, spraying explosive green diarrhea all over the streets and many of the brawlers. Within minutes, everyone was covered in blood or horse shit or a combination of both. As the street fight ebbed and flowed, the riot police started kettling the raucous crowd toward the horses and their liquid shit storm.

"This is great," I thought to myself.

The horses were shitting everywhere, and the heuristic cops were starting to beat their drums and everyone else. It made me think. Ever since the advent of artillery, straight roads have been of notable importance. When I brought Napoleon to power, we built great avenues, which he referred to as anti-riot streets. The wide straight roads allowed for cavalry charges to subdue rioters or enemies. The city planners must have created Market Street for that same purpose. Once again, I faced the slow march of horses and widespread violence. However, Richard started to falter as more elbows and assholes filled the streets.

"Beez, I'm not right. What do we do?" he asked in a panic.

I was too occupied by the onslaught of riot police, street tuffs, horse shit, and eventual tear gas that was suffocating the masses. I thought about wanding my way through the crowd to apparent safety but was determined to save Richard.

"Disperse, this is an illegal gathering!" rang out from a bull horn.

More cans of tear gas and pepper spray started affecting the brawlers' eyes and breathing as the riot police moved in with their wooden batons and gas masks, beating the MAGATS, puff boys, anti-fascists, and some innocents with impunity. Baton charging is perfectly designed to cause the maximum amount of pain to disperse the crowd. I knew that, but that's when Richard fell. Two men tripped over Richard, causing three other men to jump on him. Richard got kicked in the gut and punched several times in the back of his head, which turned him over and onto his knees.

"Beez," he cried out, looking for help.

At that moment, a gap opened in the flying wedge. Richard was on his knees when the shotgun blast caused the free-for-all to suddenly stop as the rubber bullet skimmed off the polished streetcar rail and struck him in the face, just above his left eye, fracturing his socket. Richard grabbed his face with both hands, screaming in agony. A young riot cop named Butch Hayes lowered his shield and gratuitously cracked Richard over the head with his wooden baton, opening his forehead, and leaving him very bloody, cut, and unconscious. More horses entered the fray, quickly forcing those who could stand back up Market Street. It was much like when the Vandals charged down Cortina's main street before killing my beloved Avelina.

I eventually started wanding my way towards Richard in a desperate attempt to save him, like before, with Avelina. Suddenly, a dark layer of smoke eclipsed the Sun, turning the day into night. Only a red ball could be seen through the darkened sky before ash particles started snowing down onto San Francisco. Humanity froze for a brief second, in awe or confusion, I suppose, before some wingnut screamed out: "The end is near; God has come to punish us!"

It was the perfect opportunity for the looters and vandals to commence operations. They initially set garbage cans on fire and smashed storefront windows. Expensive shops were then looted. A public bus had its windows broken out before being set ablaze.

"Get up, Richard," I said, dragging his limp body to the curb.

More bull horns were now announcing orders to disperse. The cops unleashed several canine units upon members of the puff boys carrying clubs, tearing into their flesh and rag-dolling their tattooed bodies. Many people got trampled, and one officer had his weapon snatched from his holster. The sidearm accidentally discharged in the heavy crowd, killing young Billy Anderson immediately.

Out of desperation, Captain Fairbairn called in the armored riot control vehicle with a mounted water cannon and started strip-mining the crowd into submission. As the riot began to disperse, the water cannon doused as many small garbage fires as possible. Blood, ash, and horse shit were being washed off the streets and into the gutter. Some of it puddled around the handful of limp and lifeless bodies lying in the street, including young Billy. Market Street had served its intended purpose, channeling thousands of people back from where they came.

By nightfall, the streets were empty, as much of the city was under an 8 p.m. curfew. The snatch squads were still roaming the downtown area, doing their thing, especially around the scene of the crime.

Hundreds of people were hospitalized with assorted injuries – some more critical than others. Richard had to be rushed to San Francisco General Hospital when the blood from the trauma started pooling, causing a hematoma above his left eye socket. The increased pressure on Richard's nearby brain tissue started to kill his brain cells rapidly, and poor Richard couldn't afford to lose any.

He was also of concern to the several young doctors trying to help him due to the high levels of cocaine and alcohol swimming around his vital bloodstream. One doctor said he would probably lose sight in the damaged eye and require counseling for various addictions.

"Nothing a leather eye-patch and some ice cold water couldn't fix," I said to myself.

In the morgue downstairs, Billy Anderson's parents were barely coping with reality. Their beautiful boy was on the slab with a sizable hole in his head from where the negligently discharged bullet struck him down.

"Better than an arrow," I thought. "Wrong place at the right time."

By then, the Diablo wildfire had torn through Danville, Alamo, and, over the hill, through Lafayette and Orinda. Thousands of homes and businesses were destroyed by wildfire. Hundreds of humans, livestock, and domestic pets were burned alive. Most of the horses, of course, were helped to safety.

And it all made sense. My uncle, Astaroth, landed.

IV

CHAPTER EIGHTEEN

66666666666666666666666666666666

HEALING

Time is the great healer; that's what they say anyway.

Although time never helped the past, adding insult to injury, mostly, it typically just keeps putting people in their place. When he arrived at San Francisco General Hospital, the good nurses sent him away because of the sick and injured that were already littering the halls and spilling out onto the street after the riot.

Given the madness, Richard was taken to Saint Mary's Medical center by ambulance. I suppose it was for the best because some nuns are immune to my touch, and Richard needed all the help he could get. He had undoubtedly broken some bones in his face because his left eye was already swollen shut. Richard also presented with a host of other complications.

"Sir, sir, have you consumed any drugs or alcohol in the past 24 hours?" nurse Radcliffe asked Richard while lightly patting his face.

"Has your friend been drinking?" she then turned to me and asked.

"Why do you ask?" I responded.

"Because he reeks of alcohol, is slurring his words, has clammy skin, and can't stand up," she barked at me. "If you want to help your friend, please tell me what you know; his heart rate is dropping fast."

Alcohol affects your brain and nervous system to slow your breathing, your heart rate, and other vital tasks that the human body performs. I learned that during my confusion. It was part of the curriculum. I suppose my father thought of everything. He even added the liver to keep alcohol's toxins from getting into the bloodstream. Of course, nothing, not even the liver, could have kept up with Richard last night.

"Yes, well, he had a few drinks last night and may have taken other things," I replied.

"What other things?" nurse Radcliff demanded.

"Besides the alcohol?" I asked. She just turned and gave me a stare that could only have meant yes.

"Let's see, besides the beer, wine, champagne, tequila, vodka, whiskey, and absinthe, he also ate some Vicodin and Advil," I responded. "Oh, um, he snorted some cocaine and more Vicodin. He probably also smoked cigarettes and marijuana and snorted more cocaine," I finished. "Oh, and coffee."

More stares of disgust followed, but this time the other doctors and nurses joined in. By then, Richard was starting to seize up and fall into a coma. Needles and IVs were quickly inserted into his body as the nurses and doctors sprang into action.

They gave him benzodiazepines, anticonvulsants, and other drugs with names like Carbamazepine, Divalproex, and Zonisamide. When his heart rate began dropping below average, they gave him other drugs with funny-sounding names to stimulate his epinephrine and norepinephrine. After his blood pressure skyrocketed, they gave him a different medicine. Who would have guessed flushing the human bloodstream of deadly toxins would attract such attention. When folks drank too much during my days with Nero, they ended up on the cart, deposited into a ditch, or burned. The treatment for humans who get over-served has come a long way since the old days.

After several hours of touch and go, with Richard going in and out of consciousness, the doctors and nurses finally stabilized his heart and breathing apparatus. The damage to his face and eye socket was apparent, so they put a patch over it. Fixing that would have to wait.

I was in a *Normandy Pickle* when the head nurse arrived. When you are damned if you go forward and damned if you don't, things can get precarious.

"What did you two idiots get up to last night?" she asked me while tapping Richard's arm for a vein. I felt I needed to hide our dumbfuckery and nonsense from the nurse and the doctors.

"He'll be fine, won't he?" I asked.

"Move, sir, can someone get this man outta here?" the nurse yelled.

"Will he die?" I asked.

"You need to leave now; please move," she said while butting me out of the way.

Richard was going south and quickly. By my estimation, he had no fewer than a few minutes to live. I'd seen it before; when humans get ready to die.

"Can you tell me how he got the lacerations on his butt cheeks and arms?" the nurse asked.

"He kinda had a bit of an accident," I answered.

"Oh yeah, what kind of accident?" the nurse replied.

"He fell," I said.

"Ok, well, he's gonna need a lot of stitches; looks like he landed on some glass. Is that what happened?"

"Ah, yes, he fell through a glass table," I finally divulged.

"Must have been one hell of a party," the nurse said, finally breaking a smile, rolling her eyes, and shaking her head.

"Stay with us, Richard," she persisted.

I guess the medicine worked because Richard didn't die. On the second day of his hospital stay, Richard was awake but had little memory of our Four Seasons party.

"The last thing I remember was getting shot in the face," he told Doctor Bob.

"Well, son, you are lucky to be alive, given your blood alcohol level and the numerous drugs in your system. Says here the amount of alcohol in your bloodstream was .35."

"Is that a lot?"

"It should have killed you without the other substances you took," Doctor Bob advised Richard. "Were you trying to kill yourself, Richard?" he then asked.

"I don't know, of course not, just finding my way, I guess," was his answer. "It's been hard."

You see, Richard was not always a loser. On the contrary, he was at the top of his game before I touched him.

"I'm gonna keep you here for at least a few more days," Doctor Bob informed Richard. "I can't fix your eye until the swelling goes down. In the meantime, please speak with Doctor Ross every chance you get; she can help you with finding your way."

Richard needed surgery for his fractured eye socket. He also needed help with his emotional pain. Elizabeth Bleuler-Ross was a headshrinker who would help him find his way, but let's skip ahead to the surgery.

The eye socket, or orbit, is a bony cup. It has seven different bones that contain your eyeball and all the muscles that move it. It also has tear glands, nerves, blood vessels, ligaments, and more nerves. I knew that humans shouldn't harm any part of the eye socket.

"They will not understand what they cannot see," my teacher said. "Father gave them eyes so that they could see his work, but nothing else."

A broken eye socket causes intense pain, swelling, and a black eye. The rubber bullet that struck Richard's eye had done its job. The poor man couldn't see.

"Beez, is that you?"

"Yes, my friend. It's me."

I waited up with Richard until he got carted into the operating room. Five hours later, when he came out, he was blathering about what I did not know.

"Save my boy, please, God," Richard mumbled.

Richard was coming out of surgery, still hallucinating from the anesthesia.

"Beez, do you see that?" he asked.

"See what," I replied.

To Richard, tiny green toads were hopping up and down along a slow-moving creek that flowed into a large ocean or sea. He then saw lightning bolts hitting the warm sea. As he swam toward the lightning strikes, soaked in a warm ocean, the toads started climbing up the bolts of lightning, laughing, only to jump back down into the warm salty water he floated in. Eventually, the green toads began climbing back up the bolts of heavenly lightning, sticking their tongues out, giggling, and farting. Then familiar women vividly appeared in his opium dream. They were all naked or half-dressed. His psychedelic ride kept him happy long enough for nurse Radcliffe to enter the room. Every four hours, she would stir him awake and draw a few vials of blood.

"Do you need anything for the pain?" she would ask.

Richard always replied in the affirmative.

By the fifth day, Richard broke out in hives. The opium took its toll, clotting his bowels and ravaging his nervous system. He had red itchy bumps across his back and all over his stomach. Richard had not eaten in days and was constipated. The doctors put him on a liquid diet. That's when the fun started.

More opium dreams kept him comfortable, I suppose. Strange creatures, lighting bolts, bears, and women occupied his mind. He frequently moaned while grabbing himself or just blurted out nonsensical statements in his sleep.

"I win, fucker; mom, honey, no!"

The shrink, Bleuler-Ross, would have loved it.

By the sixth day, Richard eventually came around, except for his bowels. The night nurse responsible for giving Richard his pain meds every four hours was also responsible for giving him his enema. A night potty was always placed by his bedside before the nurse inserted the tube.

"Where's Beez," he would frequently ask him.

"He comes and goes, Mr. Daily, said he had someone to meet," nurse Manny explained.

That night was very entertaining. Richard slid himself off the bed, groaning, probably hoping that his stomach and gut would fix themselves.

"Sorry, Manny, my bad," he said.

The explosion out of his ass sprayed the night nurse's shins with liquid shit, then splattered up the opposite wall. He then fell onto the porta-potty.

"Ugg, this really sucks."

"Mr. Daily, hold my hand; I got you," Manny replied, still dripping with Richard's violent discharge

Richard was trembling, shitting into the porta-potty, drunk with opiates, and somewhat blind from the surgery.

"Let's get you back in bed, sir," Manny said.

Richard then exploded for a second time all over Manny's thighs and on himself. It was a terrific mess. This routine of sorts also included two separate colonoscopies to be safe.

Finally, after eight days, Richard started eating solid foods. Jell-O, Salisbury steak, mushy peas, mashed potatoes, and ice cream. He started spending more time with Doctor Ross, opening up about his wife and son's accident.

"Do you think numbing yourself with drugs and alcohol will bring them back or change anything for the better?" Doctor Ross asked. "You didn't cause the accident."

"I wasn't there; I was always working. I barely spent any time with my son, and when I did, I was never very present, not really," Richard explained.

"Providing for your family isn't a crime, Richard," Doctor Ross suggested. "And drinking yourself to death doesn't honor their memory."

Richard went on to tell Doctor Ross about a recurrent dream or nightmare he has, how somebody magically lifted them from the vehicle moments before the semi-truck crossed over the double-yellow line.

"It wasn't your fault the truck driver fell asleep," Doctor Ross explained. "You can choose to beat yourself up, or you can decide to embrace the hurt and trust that time will eventually heal all your wounds."

"I just miss them so much, Doc," Richard said while wiping away his tears. "Have you ever lost someone you love?"

"I have," Doctor Ross answered. "My twin brother was killed in Afghanistan."

Something about that forsaken land and country. Everyone has a difficult time invading and staying alive.

"Was he in the army or something?" Richard logically asked.

"Yes, he was in special forces, but I don't know much about how or where it happened," she added.

"So, how do you deal with the pain?" Richard asked.

"By helping others cope and live through their loss," she responded. "As long as I'm moving forward with my life and helping others, I can heal along the way."

Richard closed his eye and thought about how helping others again might feel. He had helped many people solve complicated legal problems before. He was given awards for his trial advocacy and public service.

"You know, Richard, your scars will eventually fade, and your bones will grow back," Doctor Ross then added. "You just need to have some faith and believe in a brighter future."

"Maybe you're right, Doc," Richard replied. "I just don't know how to start."

"Find something or someone to love again," Doctor Ross suggested.

Then, for the first time in a long time, Richard smiled. Doctor Ross then grabbed his hand and pulled him closer for a warm embrace and a healing touch.

"Love conquers all, Richard; believe in that, and you will be fine," she said. "Start by loving yourself, and those wounds will heal."

It made sense at first, then it became quickly noticeable. Richard started to change. The mudslide of life that sent him off the path got diverted by hope and faith. Richard envisioned a direction away from recklessness, drunkenness, and despair, or maybe he just got healed by Doctor Ross' touch. I honestly don't know, but I saw the energy flowing through her body and into Richards. Maybe she was a good witch and that did not bode well for me or my plans.

"Time for a walk," I interjected. "Doctor Ross, how nice to see you again."

I gathered up poor Richard and helped him down the hall. Older people were moaning death cries and other hopeless nonsense. There was a real pain in the air.

"She's right, you know," he said to me. "The doc, she's right."

"What do you mean?" I asked.

"I need to find someone to love," Richard replied.

"Like whom?"

"It doesn't matter, Beez, just someone."

As I walked with Richard down the hospital hall in silence, we both thought about finding love again. I naturally thought about Avelina and her smell.

"Love, then, that's what you want?" I asked.

"I'm not sure, but I'm damned certain of being open to it. Besides, having a little faith won't hurt as much as a rubber bullet, now will it."

That's what my father gave humans. Faith, hope, and the ability to believe in a brighter future, regardless of how far they have fallen into despair. I wanted to feel that as well and experience a brighter future. I wanted to be in love again and share free will. As we rounded the corner and started heading back to his room, someone caught Richard's eye.

"Wait, what, no," Richard said. "Back up."

We then stared into the room where an older man was dying.

"He lost his leg, Richard; nothing more the doctors can do for him," I explained or assumed. "Come on, let's get you back in bed," I suggested.

"Delores?" Richard then said to my surprise. "It's Richard, remember me?"

It was the White Bitch, the one person who might give Richard his memory back before I took it and made him mine. You see, before my touch, Richard and Delores were soulmates and madly in love.

CHAPTER NINETEEN
66666666666666666666666666666666
REUNION AND REVELATION

When angels fall, they end up in the lowest rank of hell's hierarchy. That's where I started, back in 30 CE. I was at the lowest position amongst Satan's angels. Now, besides Lucifer and uncle Astaroth, I am the third-ranking Prince of Satan, also known as the Lord of the Flies. I even have a following. It took me two thousand years to achieve such a rank. As such, I would not allow my touch to dissolve, and my fun interrupted. It wouldn't look or sit right with Lucifer, my boss. Something needed to be done about Richard and Delores' reunion because it was stirring up old feelings.

"Nice patch, you look like shit; what a surprise," Delores said. "What the hell happened to you, Richard?"

"A lot has happened since we last spoke," Richard replied. "Nothing good, I assure you."

Richard stood at the door in silence for a while, not knowing what else to say. With so many elephants in the room, he was at a loss for words. Delores struggled to find appropriate words as well. An emotional standoff of sorts.

"Is that your...," Richard started to ask.

"My father, yes," Delores interrupted. "He got caught in the fire and had an accident."

"I remember him from our graduation. He was so friendly," Richard said without thinking. "Seems like an eternity, doesn't it?"

"Yes, a lifetime," Delores replied.

"Will he be ok?" Richard foolishly asked.

"They took his leg, hard to say," she replied, letting Richard off the stupid hook.

Richard and Delores attended law school together and partnered up for their school's moot court. Back then, they were inseparable lovers. It's been just over ten years since I took their memory and, presumably, their future when I touched Richard and then Delores for good measure. But, unfortunately, memories awaken, and my touch weakens over time. It happens when true love rears its ugly head and works as a vaccine against evil duty and pride. As I said, dad thought of everything.

"Look, Delores, I want to apologize for the other day; you're hardly recognizable, and I was not myself. I have not been well for some time," Richard truthfully explained.

Delores looked at Richard in silence as her memory poured into her thoughts. I feared she would spark the same awakening in my pupil. I needed to divide and extricate the two before my touch left their souls.

"I heard what happened to your wife and son and wanted to call, but I guess I was too busy with my own stuff or something," she replied. "I can't imagine, or, I guess, now I can, but I am truly sorry for your loss, Richard," Delores said.

Their connection was growing with each emotional exchange, making my influence weak.

"Yes, well, thank you," Richard replied. "How's your mother doing?"

Delores naturally became emotional and started to weep. It was very upsetting for me because shared emotions affect my influence, just like true love. When two people open up their hearts and expose themselves to emotional discomfort, the result is healing in nature and inoculates the soul from my touch.

"Mom didn't make it. They say she was thrown from the car," Delores sullenly explained. "Dad was eventually evacuated by helicopter and taken here."

More painful, awkward silence followed. During those moments, they kept staring at each other as the effects of my influence started to drain from their souls slowly. I was losing control of my pupil, and the feeling of paranoia overwhelmed my body.

"Richard, you should get back in bed," I instinctually suggested to break their bond.

"Give me a minute, Beez. I'm fine," he said. "Alone."

"Oh, yes, of course," I nervously responded. "I'll be in the room then."

As I walked away, I determined to touch Delores in the morning and end their reunion. One last night wouldn't cause too much harm, I decided. So, I let them have their moment.

A decision that I would later regret.

CHAPTER TWENTY
6666666666666666666666666666666666

GABRIEL BRINGS A MESSAGE:
MUCH TO ACCOMPLISH

Richard stayed with Delores for several hours that night. The more they spoke and shared, the more confusing their emotions became, given their recent past run-in with dog shit and each other.

"Do you ever think about us, Richard, after you turned into a selfish asshole?" Delores asked with a straight face.

"I don't know what or who I think about anymore," Richard replied. "It's like one big mess after I met Beez," he answered. "And some kind of stupid fuzzy blur before."

"Maybe you should spend some time by yourself and rid yourself of that peculiar man," Delores suggested. "He's no good for you, babe, and I think you know it."

But Richard only heard "babe," which stimulated his hormones and innate desires and refreshed more fond memories of Delores from before. Glimpses of moments crossed his mind, which made him think of other happy times. He became somewhat choked up with emotion and almost completely broke down crying as he sat in the chair next to Mr. Spatchcock, who was clinging to life.

"You should get some sleep," Delores said from her chair on the other side of the bed.

"Time for my medication, anyway," Richard replied. "Can I check in on you in the morning?"

"I'll be here," Delores said. "But just you, Richard."

"I'm supposed to be getting discharged tomorrow. I'll tell him not to pick me up until later in the day," Richard said. "Try and get some sleep, as well."

Delores then sat back in her chair, finding new memories. Time then traveled for her as she progressively nodded off into a deep sleep, or at least she thought she had. In her mind, a bright light burst into her dreamlike state, and the sound of a trumpet or horn filled the air. The outline in the form of a man with wings appeared backlit by the warm rays of light shining through the window. Her father then miraculously sat up and welcomed the deity.

"Blessed Robert, thou hast found favor with God; I bring you glad tidings and safe passage to heaven. Are you ready to join your soulmate in the Lord's house?" the winged man said.

"I am ready," Robert happily replied.

"And you, my child, blessed art thou among women," he turned and said to Delores.

"Who the hell are you?" she replied in a snarky manner.

"I am the archangel Gabriel, guardian of Mankind," he answered. "You must listen very carefully, believe, and have faith in what I tell you."

Delores naturally thought she was dreaming.

"Richard needs your help, Delores," Gabriel continued. "He has been touched by Beelzebub."

"Beelza, who? You mean, Richard's friend, Beez?" she replied. "Why, what, who is he anyway?"

"He is the Prince of Demons, a fallen angel now beholden to Lucifer," Gabriel answered.

"Why should I believe you?" Delores questioned.

"Because I was sent by God," Gabriel sternly responded. "Come closer, my child, let me see your hand."

Delores slowly stood up and walked toward Gabriel, but it felt like she was floating across the room in her mind.

"You shall have immunity from his touch henceforth and forever," Gabriel proclaimed. "The sign of the cross, to keep you safe and restore your faith in God," he then said while holding her right hand.

Delores felt a burning sensation on her palm as he spoke. Gabriel then put his hand on her head.

"You shall have the vision of your stolen past to help guide you and bring you joy and happiness from this day to your last," he said. "Come, child, let me show you the way."

Gabriel then grabbed both of Delores' hands and spread his wings. Significant moments in time, stolen, suddenly filled her memories. She recalled that day at the beach, when Richard got leveled by a dog blindly chasing her ball. She remembered the hours spent cramming for exams, the trip to Carmel, and the loving nights spent at her place. It was a burst of a life lived that was previously erased and forgotten.

Gabriel, through his divinity, then showed her bits and pieces of Beelzebub's time on Earth. The destruction and bloodshed he caused at first, and then the day he touched Richard - the day Beelzebub stole her happiness, joy, and future. He showed all of it and then some.

"I have seen too much bloodshed upon the Earth and the souls of too many men weep with pain and anguish," Gabriel then stated. "Richard will be the last man to suffer under Beelzebub's evil hand."

"But what can I do? I am not an angel," Dolores said. "Even if I do believe you."

Gabriel then removed a long, silver, triple-edged dagger from a metal sheath concealed under his gown.

"Take this archangel blade," he said. "It has been blessed by God."

"And do what with it?" Delores asked.

"You will act as my vessel," Gabriel explained. "Beelzebub can only be killed by taking his grace and puncturing his heart."

"What are you saying?"

"You must drain his power by slicing open his throat before he absorbs more power from the souls of Purgatory," Gabriel instructed. "His glowing red eyes will flicker and eventually turn black if you are successful."

"Then he will be dead?" Delores questioned.

"No, he will temporarily lose his power and grace. Before he absorbs more souls and regains his power, you must stab him through the heart with the blade. Only then will he be turned into dust."

Delores held the blade in her hand, examining its edges. Upon staring down the dagger's business end, she noticed that its cross-section showed a three-pointed star. Delores wondered if she could commit such an act of violence and questioned if she could kill in cold blood.

"Why me, why don't you kill him yourself?" she then asked, looking for a way out.

"He will know I'm coming. Archangels and fallen angels still sense each other's grace. You must trick Beelzebub to gain his confidence and get close enough to use the blade," Gabriel said. "I suspect he will be coming for you to keep Richard's soul."

"Me, why me?"

"True love weakens his influence, my child, and you and Richard belong together," Gabriel explained. "He will not know you have been touched by an angel and have become immune to his touch. So now go, with God as your ally and fulfill your rightful destiny."

The room then exploded with a burst of blue and white light. The same backlit outline in the shape of a winged man appeared at the window, then disappeared into itself as if to be sucked into a black hole. Likewise, the sound of a trumpet or horn blew loudly and then progressively faded into what became periodic beeps.

Beep, beep, beep....beep.... beep ever slowly went the heart rate monitor measuring her father's heart rhythm and oxygen saturation as Delores slowly woke from her realistic dream.

Beep, beep, b————————————flatline. Dead.

Bob Spatchcock's heart flatlined the machine's troughs and crests. Before Delores realized she was back among mortals, nurses and doctors poured into his room and began frantically working to jumpstart his heart.

"Charging...five hundred...clear!"

Delores watched her father's body violently convulse from the electrical current passing through his chest and heart. Finally, however, the tireless blood pump stopped beating, cutting off the life-sustaining oxygen from his brain. The doctor then asked for more gel to be placed on the paddles.

"Charging...seven hundred...clear!"

Bob's lifeless body jumped off the bed again. The doctor pushed down on his chest several times and checked for a pulse. But, unfortunately, nothing more could be done to save him.

"Let's call it; the time is 11:46 a.m."

The room went temporarily silent after resuscitation efforts failed. The doctors and nurses were all staring at Delores as if to say we did our best. But Delores didn't feel anguish or gut-wrenching sadness at all. Delores knew Gabriel took her father's soul and, hopefully, reunited it with her mother's. She grabbed his hand and held it tight for one last time. Bob Spatchcock lay silent with a tiny smile on his face. Delores knew he was at peace in the house of the Lord. Then panic set in.

"What time did you say it was?" she asked the Doctor.

"11:46," he replied.

"11:46, how can that be," Delores questioned.

Before the doctor responded, Delores kissed her father on the forehead and bolted out the door. People act in many strange ways after losing a loved one, so the doctors and nurses didn't think it to be too abnormal.

"Excuse me, nurse, what room is Richard Daily staying in?" she asked while fast-walking down the hallway. "He was released this morning," the nurse replied. "Mr. Daily left with his friend."

Delores then slowed her pace and eventually stopped in her tracks. A surge of willful determination then crisscrossed through her body.

"Mother fuck," she cried out at first. "The angel blade," she then said out loud to herself before running back to her father's room.

A few nurses were unplugging her father from the various machines and pulling the many tubes inserted into his veins when she entered the room.

"Do you need a minute alone with your father, dear?" the nurse asked.

"Yes, please, if you don't mind," Delores responded.

127

She followed the nurses out and closed the door behind them. When she grabbed the doorknob, she felt a slight irritation on her right palm. She reactively turned it over and saw a small raised crucifix burned into her skin.

"You shall have immunity from his touch henceforth and forever," she repeated Gabriel's words to herself.

Delores walked over to the window where she had seen the light and looked out upon the smoke-filled sky choking San Francisco and beyond. Her mind began to race with visions of driving the angel blade into Beelzebub's evil heart.

"The angel blade," she repeated to herself.

Delores turned and scoured the room, then paused in thought. Was it all a vivid dream? The burn on her palm didn't think so, but where was the powerful blade? Delores slumped into the chair where she had dreamed the entire encounter with Gabriel. Maybe the burn on her palm was just a freaky coincidence or nervous rash, she considered.

"Be logical, Delores," she said to herself. "Angels and demons are just fairytales."

Even still, she dug through her purse, looking for the ancient blade, and found nothing.

"See, you're not going mad," she thought.

Eventually, Delores gathered herself and let the nurses back in to finish preparing her father for the morgue. His body would come to rest in the Spatchcock family plot next to his father and the urn that contained most of Judy's ashes and the neighbor's juniper bush. Delores would have remained paralyzed, not knowing what to do next, but for the tell-tale growl coming from her stomach. She also worried about Richard, not convinced that what she had experienced the long night before was just a dream.

"Nothing a good lunch and a bottle of wine won't cure," she said to herself. "Nurse, I'll be back later to make arrangements for my father."

The death of important or famous people usually marks the end of an era. The finality of death also acts as a milepost for the road yet traveled without that person. Delores found herself at a crossroad and didn't know which route to take. If her encounter with Gabriel was real, she needed to take the more difficult and less traveled road to save Richard. However, if Delores determined to stay on the same path as before her father's death, and before the firestorm, and without the blade, then she would be mired in doubt and never ending confusion. It was a conundrum for her that presented no immediate solution until she walked out of the hospital.

"Excuse me, sir, can you recommend a decent restaurant nearby?" Delores asked the old man sitting at the front desk.

"What are you hungry for?" he replied.

"Mostly wine," she replied with a forced smile, wanting to be drunk.

"In that case, make your way to Tadich Grill," he said. "Try the sole."

Delores had eaten there hundreds of times before, but thanked the old man nonetheless.

"I already called you a cab," he informed her. "It's waiting for you outside."

"But I didn't…how did you…do I know you?" Delores asked somewhat confused.

"I'm a friend of Gabriel's," he replied. "He thought I should keep this safe for you."

The old man then handed Delores an old wooden box with strange writings, maybe Hebrew, Greek, or Latin. She instinctively looked over her shoulder at first, then accepted the wooden box.

"Who are you again?" she asked.

"I am Raphael," he replied. "Now go with God; you have much to accomplish."

Delores opened the box to reveal the archangel blade she saw in her dream, then quickly closed the box. "Oh, Jesus God," she said out loud, capturing the attention of several people in the lobby.

"Mam, are you ok?" a stranger asked.

Delores turned and made up some plausible response.

"Me, um, of course, Raphael here just, um, startled me, but, yes, I'm fine, I think."

"Who?" the stranger asked.

Delores turned back toward the desk and saw nothing more than a white feather sitting on the counter. It puffed into the air and landed. Raphael was gone, vanished into thin air. She then pushed and picked up the newfound feather, then clutched it.

"Time to go; it's time to go, isn't it," she announced. "Ha, I have much to accomplish, don't I."

Delores seemed crazy in her speech, then turned abruptly and marched out of the hospital.

"Much to accomplish, sir, much to accomplish."

CHAPTER TWENTY-ONE

BACK TO CHURCH

Delores Spatchcock was a lousy Catholic, but not like you think. Growing up, the Spatchcocks regularly attended Sunday Mass. As a young girl, she found the smell of older men funny and would point them out during Catholic service.

"Daddy, that man smells funny," she would say out loud while hanging off the back of the church pew.

Delores possessed a logical mind from a very young age.

"Daddy, why are the poos so uncomftabull?"

Her father sympathized with Delores regarding the lack of ergonomics and the uncomfortable nature of church pews. He believed that the devil designed the bench. Practically speaking, it served the Church's overarching goals because most Christians would pray to God to relieve themselves from the inevitable back pain they suffered after sitting through a lengthy mass. The Holy Spirit and the church pew, like Pius kneeling, helped believers in the mortification of the sins of the flesh when they lacked the spiritual discipline for self-flagellation. Nonetheless, Bob kept his mouth shut to avoid Judy's wrath should he side with young Delores' pranks and restive nature.

Because Delores could not sit still for a minute, she spent most of her time crawling along the floor in between the pews or playing make-believe with her toy horse up and down her father's leg and arm. Her mother was the disciplinarian and enforcer in general, especially during Sunday Mass. The toy horse was always snatched from her little hand first, followed by a stern look. However, in response, she never pouted or cried, but upped her campaign to embarrass and annoy her extremely devout mother.

"You smell funny," she would repeat to the old man sitting behind her father.

"Delores!" her mother would firmly whisper, pinching Bob, before yanking her back down.

The idle threats of withholding donuts after Mass would then be applied.

"But daddy promised," she would say in response, wisely playing her father's unconditional love against her mother's disdain and impatience to get what she wanted.

At first, Delores used her innocence as a weapon against her mother's insistence on attending Sunday Mass. When her innocence started to fade, and Judy started to gain the upper hand, Delores would find new and better ways to embarrass her mother in order to get carried out of the church by her father. The most effective and final straw being the kid fart.

By the time she reached the first grade, Delores regularly spent Sunday Mass in the church's playground so that her mother could pray in peace, the first of many small victories in the psychological war between mother and daughter. As she progressed through elementary school, Delores occasionally appeased her mother by attending church on Christmas Eve and Easter Sunday, but only after winning enough of the lesser battles.

Delores graduated from high school at the top of her class. After which, she completely broke free from Mother Judy's pursuit of devotion, leaving behind the scars of an 18-year-old religious tug of war between them.

· · · · · · · · · ·

Saint Ignatius Church was the first thing Delores saw after walking out of the hospital with "much to accomplish." She stared at the large twin spires and impressive dome for many minutes before making her decision to return to church.

Saint Ignatius is the church on the University of San Francisco campus and dominates the hilltop in San Francisco's exact center. The church has a mix of Italian Renaissance and some Baroque architecture. It's the City's Jesuit headquarters and serves as a parish of the Catholic Archdiocese of San Francisco.

As luck or possibly divine intervention would have it, Father Dante Pulido took confession on that day. He was a Jesuit and visiting professor of philosophy for the University. That's what he told everyone, anyway. Father Pulido also dabbled in exorcism. He entered the Society of Jesus in 1965 and was ordained into the priesthood in 1975.

As with all Society of Jesus members, Father Pulido had served in many dangerous, worn-torn locations as a young priest. Like Saint Ignatius, Father Pulido had military training, serving in Vietnam and Central America. He liked to refer to himself colloquially as "God's marine." On loan from the General Curia in Rome, Father Pulido came perfectly equipped for Delores' confession.

"Bless me, Father, um, it's been forever since my last confession, and I know I have probably sinned hundreds of times, but I need your help," she began.

"Good morning. How may the Lord help you to confess your sins?" Father Pulido responded.

"I think it's more of a request on his part, Father. Um, I was visited by an angel last night, before he took my father. It was Gabriel, then Raphael," Delores struggled to explain. "My friend, Richard, he is in trouble or cursed, I don't know."

"Give thanks to the Lord, for he is good," Father Pulido said without hearing Delores'pleas for help.

"For Christ's sake, you're not listening!"Delores shouted. "Do you get many angels visiting your flock, Father?" she facetiously asked. "And what's that horrible smell?"

Father Pulido remained quiet until the confessional door slowly swung open, and he held out his hand.

"Come with me, child, you can pray for an Act of Contrition another day."

Father Pulido led Delores into an alcove located at the church's front, then sat her down on an antique pew that had survived the 1906 earthquake and fire. She went on to describe the light and the trumpet and the image of a man with wings. Delores showed Father Pulido the archangel blade, and the raised sign of the cross burned into her palm. She told him about Richard and Beelzebub's hold on his soul and Gabriel's instructions for saving Richard's soul.

"He says I must cut his throat and then drive the blade into his heart to send him back to hell."

Father Pulido sat in silence, absorbing Delores' story. He closed his eyes and began to pray or possibly examine his conscience silently. Delores naturally felt the uncomfortable church pew underneath her again and began to fidget and revert to her childhood ways.

"So, will you help me, Father?" she asked, interrupting Father Pulido's meditative state.

After a deep sigh, Father Pulido began to pray out loud:

Hail Mary, full of grace,
the Lord is with you;
Blessed are you among women,
and blessed is the fruit of your womb, Jesus.
Holy Mary, Mother of God,
Pray for us sinners now
and at the hour of our death. Amen.

"What do you have that he wants?" Father Pulido then opened his eyes and asked Delores.

"What do I have? Nothing that I can think of, Father," she replied. "My soul, I guess," she speculated.

"There are many of those, my dear. We need something individual, something unique," Father Pulido explained. "Beelzebub has an excessive, disordered love of material things and even more perverse love of harming other beings."

"How do you know that?" Delores replied. "How does that help us?"

"Because he won't be able to help himself," Father Pulido answered Delores' second question. "Beelzebub has always put his wants, urges, desires, and fanciful whims before all else."

Ignoring his lack of complete response, Delores continued with her inquiry.

"So, by taking something of value of his, we can kill him?" she asked.

"Not exactly, but Pride goeth before destruction," Father Pulido answered. "We need to lure him into a place where he won't suspect he is in mortal danger."

"I am immune to his touch now, right? Gabriel said Richard and I are destined to be together, true love and all that nonsense," Delores said out loud.

"Yes, angels such as Gabriel are never wrong on matters of the human heart," Father Pulido replied. "Are you not in love with Richard?"

"I once was, but that was a long time ago. Why does it matter?"

"Because your love for Richard will weaken Beelzebub's influence over him, and that will damage his pride," Father Pulido explained. "He is too arrogant to let that happen."

"What if Richard doesn't love me anymore?"

"That is where you must have faith in God's plan and place trust in his angel's divine guidance."

Delores began to pace about the alcove searching her soul for the faith her mother tried so hard to instill in her as a child. She began to weep as the reality of her parents' deaths, the destruction of her childhood home, and the task placed before her overwhelmed her emotions.

"I don't even know what love feels like anymore, Father," she said with uncomfortable, crying laughter. "Why is this happening to me?"

"Only God knows the why, Delores. It is up to you to decide whether or not to trust his judgment and choose the righteous path to save Richard's soul."

After more silence, Father Pulido led Delores down another proverbial path.

"Are you sure there is nothing of value that Richard has that we can use to trick Beelzebub?" he asked. "Next to pride, he suffers from inexhaustible greed."

Delores gathered her emotions, closed her eyes, and started to search for any helpful memory from the past few days. Flashes of time and events bombarded her mind: the firestorm, the riot, the ashen red sky, and her father's death. She then began to recall the night Richard arrived at the hospital. She watched him roll by her father's room in a gurney with all sorts of tubes dripping life-saving liquid into his body. Beelzebub followed an unconscious Richard and the nurses into the room down the hall. Later, in the middle of the night, she crept into Richard's room to confirm it was him. He was alone. Delores remembered the darkness and smell of alcohol overwhelming her senses. If not for the bright red numbers on the monitor, the periodic beeps, and the green wave-like patterns, she would have been entirely in the dark.

"Richard, what the hell happened to you?" she remembered whispering while sitting down next to his bed.

After some time sitting in silence, however, she felt compelled to grasp his hand and lean forward to kiss his forehead. As she slid to the edge of her seat, her feet naturally slid underneath.

"What the hell do you have in here?" she recalled saying to herself.

Delores reached underneath the chair and pulled the candy-apple red and gold *Ironman* backpack up onto her lap. Being naturally curious and amused, she patted the outside of the pack and then unzipped the main compartment.

"Holy shit!"

Delores pulled out a few bricks of cash, then dug through the remainder until she reached the bottom. There was just under $120,000 left.

"What have you gotten yourself into, my love?" she thought.

Delores put the money back and slid the backpack under the seat. Her memory then went dark except for the silhouette of a man standing at the door.

· · · · · · · · · ·

"Ironman!" she yelled out to Father Pulido.

"What about him?" he replied.

"There was an Ironman backpack full of cash," she explained to Father Pulido. "I remember now. Richard had at least $100,000 or more stuffed in a kids backpack."

"You're just now telling me this?" Father Pulido questioned. "Where is it now?"

"How the hell should I know? It must still be with Richard, I guess," Delores cursed. "There was a man that appeared in the doorway that night. After he appeared, I don't remember much, but I'm certain of the money."

"Undoubtedly Beelzebub," Father Pulido said. "You must not delay your destiny any further, my child. Go to him. Seduce him if you must, but stop sleeping under these strange skies. Find a way back into his heart."

"What are you saying? You think I can just show up at his doorstep and ask him to take me back and, oh, by the way, where's the fucking money, honey," Delores sarcastically replied. "This is all mixed up."

"I do not claim to know the tools of your trade, Delores, but I do know men," Father Pulido replied with a hint of misogyny. "Maybe you should use those God-given gifts I see and let nature take its course."

Delores fought back her ardent feminism, sitting in pensive silence. She had fought sexism all her adult life, especially during her professional career. Father Pulido's age and apparent profession, however, diluted the effect of his words.

"I'll let that go for the sake of Richard," she said. "I'm just an old friend showing kindness, right, Father?"

"Love and kindness are never wasted and may very well save Richard's soul, Delores," Father Pulido preached. "Go to him and find that backpack."

"What if Beelzebub is with him? Should I take the angel blade just in case?" Delores asked.

"No, leave it with me. The church will need to inspect the artifact for its authenticity," he replied.

"Oh, ah, ok, and Beelzebub, what am I supposed to do about him?"

"For now, leave Beelzebub up to me. He and I have unfinished business."

Delores squinted with confusion and naturally felt the need to cross examine Father Pulido about his response. But she also felt compelled to find Richard and hopefully reopen his heart. With her stomach growling even louder, she wished Father Pulido well.

"Good luck with that, Father," she said with a firm handshake. "I'll be in touch."

"So will I, Delores Spatchcock, now go with God."

CHAPTER TWENTY-TWO
66666666666666666666666666666666666
MY MEETING WITH ASTAROTH

The first thing you notice when Astaroth enters the room is his foul-smelling breath. Somehow, it hits you like a hard-charging horse before the second thing you smell – his disgusting body odor. Even still, you best not joke about it because he is a grand duke, next in line to the throne and treasurer of hell. He keeps an accounting of all the lost souls down below and the number of new souls we fallen angels send to hell. In my opinion, apart from the power he wields, Astaroth has the personality of a cucumber.

Before his fall, Astaroth was a promising angel. He was skilled in mathematics, science, and arts and crafts. Astaroth especially liked arts and crafts. During his confusing period, Astaroth used to sew the heads of chickens onto vampire bats and watch them starve to death after losing the means to drink blood. He kept hundreds of vampire bats and chickens for his favorite arts and crafts project. He called them *chattens* or *backens* – I forget.

Astaroth finally crossed the line, however, when he sewed the head of one of God's favorite and cherished Lynxes to a mini pot-bellied pig and named him "Oiskers." To this day, he loves to talk about Oiskers and still complains that God unfairly punished him and that someday he will be restored to his rightful place in heaven.

At first, I paid little attention to his note summoning me to the angel portal where Furland Monroe, Dickie Smits, and Earl

James met their horrible demise. I didn't do that. Astaroth came raging down upon Earth, kicking up the flames that ate the fuel, not me. Nonetheless, I figured it was an unannounced checkup or forgotten annual review. It has been a while since the boss sent an agent, I determined. Either way, the note, written in Latin, provided little or no information about his intent.

Astaroth wrote: *Occursum in Diablo porta, dominica meridie.* Simple translation: *Meet at Diablo portal, Sunday at noon.*

Mount Diablo looked like a moonscape, except for Furland's burnt truck, the lifeless oak trees, and the coordinate markings where the lightning bolt first struck Earth. Typically, as we called them, *travel scars* left a cross-section of a sphere with pentagonal lines inside the circle and unique symbols that served as compass headings. From a birds-eye-view, travel scars are visible at various locations around the planet, and they are all different. Desert markings in Kazakhstan and Nevada, crop circles near Stonehenge, strange-shaped lakes, and specific circular rock carvings, like the one left by Astaroth's arrival, are all travel scars from angels, both fallen and heavenly.

"Dear uncle, what brings you to town? I wish I could say it's a pleasure to see you," I snarked. "Still searching for that lost bar of soap?"

"Very funny, Beez, still playing games, I see," he replied. "The boss sent me."

"I'm fallen, uncle; why on earth does he care?"

"The other boss, Beez. You're short, very short on souls."

"By the looks of it, uncle, you took care of that. I have never seen such death and destruction since Nero burned Rome to the ground," I replied while pointing west. "What do you want? I'm busy and have things to do."

"I arrived on the second bolt, Beez. A coincidence. The first one was all mother nature's doing," he explained. "Humans need to tend to their house, as do you, Beez."

"Strange coincidence, uncle. Will you be here long?"

Astaroth then let out a putrid growl, clearing his throat.

"As long as it takes," he replied. "Your pupil, Richard Daly, is not enough," he remarked. "Such petty games must stop."

"But I like games, especially with humans. Why do you care who I play with anyway?"

Astaroth then grew red, shooting a foul green gooey liquid from his nose.

"Stealing money and playing with fools is not the work of angels, stupid boy!" he said. "When will you get that? Besides, she already has taken your power."

"What are you saying, uncle?"

"You've done well, Beez, for many thousands of years," he said.

"When it suited me," I replied. "I'm good at what I do."

"Yes, yes, but now she has taken Richard's love back, and she might even have stolen your money," he replied.

"She? Do you mean Delores? I touched her days ago. The money is safe."

"Are you sure? His soul is bleeding love for the woman, and the last time I checked, the money was gone."

"Don't be a fool, Astaroth, I'm still the prince down here, and no human can trick me," I said. "Besides, I can touch him whenever I want. It's my choice."

"But what if it isn't your choice? What if you no longer have the touch over him?" he asked.

"That would be impossible, uncle. I am too smart for that to happen," I replied.

Astaroth then scraped the ground with his sharp talons, partially erasing the angel scar from his arrival.

"But what if you are wrong? What if you made a mistake?" he questioned my better judgment and ability.

"I am never wrong about humans, uncle. They do as I say, with my help. That's what makes them human," I said. "How do you know about the cash?"

"A little birdy, Beez, a little birdy," he replied.

"Who is this little birdy, uncle? The cash is mine," I asked.

"It doesn't matter who. The boss demands new souls, and you need to give him some," he replied. "You've had your fun with Richard. Time to let him go."

The thought of letting him go would give the impression that Astaroth was right and that I was wrong. Such impressions were not a part of my being. I could not accept failure on any level, especially if it meant that a human would be the cause of my defeat. Richard was mine and so was the money. To give in to Astaroth's demands would necessarily deprive me of my fun, and that was something I could never do.

"I'll give it some thought," I said to appease Astaroth. "He's not going anywhere for some time, anyway."

"Why? Where are you keeping him?" he asked.

"I'm not keeping him. He's healing from his painful wounds at his home," I said with a smile. "But I will keep an eye on him, dear uncle, rest assured."

Despite my witty humor attempts, Astaroth just turned his back and dragged his claws along the scorched sandstone.

"I'll be in touch, Beez. Do try and humble yourself, son. I hate being the bearer of bad news."

Before I could ask him what he meant, Astaroth was gone. Naturally, I paid no attention to his words of wisdom and advice. How dare he suggest I was wrong or mistaken. I am never wrong. No one is better than me. I take what I want even if I don't need it.

"The money is mine!" I shouted at the empty sky. "I am never wrong!"

CHAPTER TWENTY-THREE
6666666666666666666666666666666666
THAT IDIOM DETECTIVE

Detective Tawni Franks arrived at Richard's house in Tiburon at 9:00 am. The early bird gets the worm, she frequently said. Tawni Franks grew up in the South, in Natchez, on the banks of the Mississippi River. Like most Southerners, she spoke slowly with prolonged vowels, which gave her a distinct southern drawl. It has been said, mainly by Tawni, that she will search high and low with a fine-tooth comb to find a needle in a haystack. Her southern charm would disarm you at first, and then her shapely, athletic figure would mesmerize you until her southern drawl and perfect white smile would have you eating out of the palm of her hand.

"Good morning, Mr. Daly; my name is Detective Tawni Franks. I'm with the San Francisco Police Department. We spoke on the phone the other day" she started. "You poor little thing, by the looks of it, the sticks and stones have already done their worst. You look like you've been ridden hard and put up wet. Remember, dear; It is always darkest before the dawn. Can I come in?"

Tawni always started off her interviews with a mouthful of idioms, proverbs and southern expressions. She believed it made her less intimidating and lowered her suspect's guard.

"As I told you on the phone, I don't remember much before the riot and my injuries," Richard replied. "Can I get you anything?"

"Much obliged, Mr. Daly. I'm fine. As I said, I am investigating the death of Larry George. I believe you were with him the day he died," she said. "At Scooter Rebock's, is that right?"

"I don't know him that well. He was there the same time I was," Richard replied.

"What did y'all talk about? Did he seem upset or worried?" Tawni asked. "I always like to hear it straight from the horse's mouth."

"I think he was having problems at home. He didn't say," Richard responded. "Maybe money problems, I can't say for sure."

"Were y'all with anybody else? I just need to know which way the wind is blowing."

"Yes, my friend, Beez, was with us at the bar," Richard revealed. "Have you spoken to him?"

"Not yet, Mr. Daly, I'll cross that bridge when I come to it," she replied. "For now, I'm trying to wrap my head around how Mr. George ended up with his head split open on the sidewalk below his boss's flat on Eddy Street."

"I wish I knew, Ms. Franks. Your guess is as good as mine," Richard said.

"Richard, honey, I like to give most people the benefit of the doubt, so let's stop beating around the bush," Tawni replied. "You see, I have video surveillance of you and Mr. Beez walking down Eddy Street right after poor Larry met his demise. Birds of a feather, Mr. Daly, birds of a feather."

"Yes, I think we got burritos at *El Mono Cantor*," Richard recalled. "I go there frequently."

"You said, *we*, Mr. Daly. Do you mean you and Larry?"

"No, Beez and myself. That's what I remember."

Detective Franks started to search through her messy briefcase, deliberately mumbling nonsense to herself as she flipped through graphic pictures of dead Larry George. Sometimes the shock of seeing mangled body parts, especially spilled brain matter, gets people talking. Richard, however, didn't seem to bite. So, Tawni tossed him a curveball.

"Do you own a gun, Mr. Daly?" she asked. "My daddy taught me to shoot on the banks of the Mississippi River. We used to shoot tin cans off old fence posts," she rambled on.

"No, I mean yes, not really," Richard replied. "I bought my son a .22 years ago, but it's been in storage since. His mother disapproved."

"Is that his backpack? I love Ironman," she then asked while pointing at the empty pack.

"Oh, ah, no, one of the neighbor kids must have left it out front. My son passed away several years ago."

"Oh, you poor thing. I am so very sorry for your loss. God's little angels."

"Thank you. But, why do you ask?"

"Oh, I'm not supposed to let the cat out of the bag. However, God hates a coward. Anyway, did you know the coroner dug a strange old bullet out of Larry's chest? Forensics is examining the slug as we speak. Any idea how that might have got there?"

"How should I know," Richard said while adjusting his eye patch. "I thought he fell or killed himself or something."

"He certainly fell, and that probably killed him, but what came first, the chicken or the egg," she replied. "In my experience, it takes two to tango, Mr. Daly."

"I'm not following you, Detective. Have you recovered the gun?" Richard asked.

"I'm not allowed to spill the beans about an ongoing investigation, Mr. Daly. Do you know anyone else that might have wanted to harm Mr. George?"

Richard immediately thought of the Scattuzzo brothers but had enough sense to hold his tongue. The money could provide detective Franks the necessary "motivation" and *why* someone killed Larry George. Even though Richard was technically innocent of murder, he felt mixed up in a criminal conspiracy with Beelzebub. Despite his foggy memory, after they took the money, he undoubtedly was involved in some crime.

"I couldn't say, Ms. Franks."

"What about Antoinette Archambault?"

"Who?"

"Your bartender friend, Mr. Daly. I believe she goes by Tony."

"What possible motive would she have?" Richard asked.

"The oldest one in the book. Money," detective Franks replied. "Or maybe I'm barking up the wrong tree. What do you think?"

Richard began to feel edgy and uncomfortable as Tawni slowly circled. She intentionally threw out false theories to goad Richard into making a mistake. He certainly felt compelled to defend Tony out of self-preservation. What if she knew about Tony's specials? Did they already perform an autopsy? Did she know about Larry's gambling addiction? All of it raced through Richard's mind as Tawni stared into his eyes and smiled.

"I don't see how Tony would have any reason to want Larry dead, Ms. Franks," Richard said.

"Neither do I, Richie. For all I care, all y'all can order as many specials as y'all want; they're your brain cells, after all," Tawni divulged.

Richard played stupid at her revelation.

"I don't know what you're talking about, detective. Is there anything else I can help you with today? I'm starting to feel under the weather," he said, hoping to end the interview.

"I think that's enough for today. I know where to find you if something comes up," Tawni said as she gathered up her pictures and papers and reports. However, as she stood up, Tawni deliberately dropped a mugshot of Mario Scattuzzo.

"Oh, speak of the devil, I almost forgot," she said. "Do you recognize this man?"

Richard briefly looked at the photo without grabbing it and summoned the fortitude to quell his stomach from turning into knots. The only person that could place him at the penthouse was now in the hands of his charming adversary.

"No, he doesn't look familiar," he said. "Why do you ask?"

"Oh, I'm just trying to kill two birds with one stone," Tawni replied. "His brother, Dante, reported him missing the day after Larry flung himself off the roof and shot himself on the way down," she sarcastically informed Richard. "Are you sure you've never seen this man, Richie?"

Richard adjusted his patch again and shifted in his seat.

"I'm positive, will that be all?"

"Let's let sleeping dogs lie, for now, Richie. You get some rest," Tawni responded. But, as she walked out the front door, she grabbed the last word.

"You want some good advice, Richie? My daddy always said, don't put all your eggs in one basket. Do you know what that means?"

"I never really thought about it much," Richard replied. "Should I?"

"It means what you're doing is too risky," she said. "The devil is in the details, Richie. There's no such thing as a free lunch.

Are you catching my drift? Anyway, I sure do hope you know what you're doing."

Richard closed the door behind Detective Franks and walked toward his hidden guest.

"So do I, detective Franks, so do I."

· · · · · · · · · ·

"For Christ's sake, I thought she would never leave. Do you think she knows about the money?"

"How the hell should I know? She must know something. You better pack it up and get out of here before Beez shows up."

"Just remember what I told you and stick with the plan."

"Are you sure this is the right thing to do?" Richard asked.

"It's the only way to get our lives back. Have faith, my love. It has to work."

Richard pulled her close and kissed her on the forehead.

"Whatever happens, thank you for last night; I remember everything, now."

"I love you too, *Richie*. Now listen to your new girlfriend, Taaawni, and get some rest."

Delores kissed Richard on the lips and departed for San Francisco with Beelzebub's money and a plan.

CHAPTER TWENTY-FOUR
6666666666666666666666666666666666666
ANGER AND ARROGANCE

Aristotle once told me that, *Anybody can become angry – that is easy, but to be angry with the right person and to the right degree and at the right time and for the right purpose, and in the right way – that is not within everybody's power and is not easy.*

It's a mouthful, I know. But Totes was like that. A real thinker.

Nonetheless, after my meeting with uncle Astaroth, I got to thinking. He had ruffled my wings somewhat. Despite his smell, I respected Astaroth enough to let his words of advice begin to fester inside me. I sat down next to Furland's melted truck and allowed myself to become bothered. After a while, it turned into mild annoyance, then eventual anger. I couldn't let it go, wouldn't let it go. Despite that feeling, in hindsight, I should have taken a long walk up the hill toward the summit or just listened to my famous uncle Astaroth.

"But what if you're wrong? What if you made a mistake?" he did say, and it rubbed me wrong. I, naturally, take great pride in my work. The suggestion that Delores Spatchcock stole one of my souls was unacceptable, if not unbearable. The very thought of her stealing my money, of course, made me temporarily insane.

"ASTAROTH!" I screamed at the heavens. But it fell on deaf ears, especially mine. You see, I forebear reason for anger and mistake for excuse and pride for shame. Even still, given those apparent faults, no human should prove me wrong—most of all and certainly not Delores Spatchcock or her old lover, Richard Daly.

· · · · · · · · · ·

"You don't look well at all, Richard. I thought you were healing?" I said to him when I arrived at his house in Tiburon. Upon my arrival, I left an angel scar on the hill above his home because I could.

"People get better, Beez. It just takes time. Where have you been?" Richard replied.

"Where have I been?" I repeated. "Let's not worry about that, partner. Where's the money?" I immediately asked.

Richard smiled, most unexpectedly. I could touch him at any moment, I thought, but his smile threw me. Too confident, I surmised. Maybe I'll listen, this time, I said to myself.

"Don't you think we should double it?" he then asked. "Have another party, maybe?"

I could tell by his glib tone and disheartened manner that he was being facetious. I need to give him a touch-up, I thought. In the past, there was never any question about the fun. All of my past pupils were degenerates, accepting of my touch. Nero, Vlad, Leo, Max, Addy, and Joey all loved to take my gifts, especially Addy – to a fault, of course. But despite that one mishap with Addy, they all loved to party. "Let's have some fun, Beez," they all said. Maybe that's what made me so upset and angry. Things were changing. Perhaps, today, Richard was starting to piss me off.

"What are you talking about, Richie? Let's grab the money and have some fun," I said. "Where's the money anyway?" I quickly added.

"Good news, Beez. Glad you asked," he replied. "Hold on."

"What? Just get it, and let's have some fun. A new hotel, maybe," I offered.

Richard then shushed me and asked me to follow him into his kitchen.

"Coffee?" he asked.

"No, thank you. Richard, what have you done with my money?" I repeated in a more forceful tone.

"I gave it to Delores. She has an investment guy who can clean it up and possibly double it in the process. She's throwing in $50 000 of her own money," he replied. "I thought we could both meet with him on Wednesday."

"Meet with who? Richard. You didn't give my money to Delores, the white bitch," I questioned. "Have you lost your mind?" I yelled.

"Well, it isn't our money, Beez, not really," he flippantly replied.

In response, I almost wanded Richard through the sliding glass door into his pool.

"Of course, it's our money, Richard. Dead men have no use for money," I pointed out.

"I agree, but their widows do," he calmly replied. "He had kids, Beez."

The nonchalant morality of his response raised my concern that Astaroth was possibly telling the truth. Impossible, I immediately thought to myself. Richard didn't suddenly become immune to my touch. Or did he?

"Who has my money? I want to see him tomorrow, Richard, not Wednesday; tomorrow!" I yelled. "Call him or call Delores, I don't care but do what you gotta do to make tomorrow happen."

"Sure, Beez, I'll call Delores this evening. By the way, you know that detective is looking for you. This morning, she came here asking a lot of questions about Larry and the Scatuzzo brother that left the money. She said Larry got shot."

"What detective?"

"Tawni Franks. Detective Tawni Franks. She's going to be a southern pain in our ass if you don't talk to her. She needs to go away," Richard replied.

"What do you mean? What's a southern pain in our ass?" I asked.

"You'll see. Give Detective Franks a call and talk to her. We were never at the penthouse," he replied.

"Yes, of course, I'll tou…I mean, call her in the morning and give her a statement. In the meantime, call Delores and set an appointment for tomorrow afternoon. I want my money back, Richard."

"Whatever you say, Beez. You're the boss," Richard said.

"That's right; I'm the boss. See you tomorrow."

· · · · · · · · · ·

"Hi, it's me. Can you talk?"

"Of course, what did he say? Did he buy it?"

"He's pissed. He wants to meet you guys tomorrow. Did you talk to Father Pulido? Is he going to help us?"

"Yes, we can use my office. What time?"

"I don't know; how about the end of the day after everyone leaves?"

"Ok, five then?"

"I'll be there, my love."

"Oh, and Richard?"

"Yes, Delores."
"I love you too."

CHAPTER TWENTY-FIVE
6666666666666666666666666666666666
LOVE AND REINCARNATION

In 54 CE, an Apostle named Paul wrote letters to his Christian disciples in Corinth, Greece. He was an acquaintance of mine and a devoted missionary promoting the Christian faith – I let it slide when I was not with Nero.

Paul traveled a lot back then, even more than me, writing his bothersome letters to his flock along the way. His best work was about Love. He preached that love wasn't envious or boastful, or arrogant. Paul believed love is kind and patient. He assured me that Love never ends, but different minds, set against each other, tend to disagree.

Around 58 CE, when Paul and I were drinking in Ephesus, he picked a fight with a non-believer.

"Beez," he said with blood dripping from his nose, "If God is for us, who can be against us?"

He was a true captain and leader, the kind of man that was the first one in and the last guy out of every dust-up. He also gave good speeches—typical captain. After the fight, where we mostly won, he said to me, "it's not how good you are; it's how bad you want it."

Paul throttled a guy's nose and gave more than he received on that day. I had to give it to Paul; he was determined and sturdy and complete. I admired his talented left hook and unending stamina in the fight as well. During the brawl, Paul did the lion's share of the fighting with the non-believers, as all captains do. At one point, during the fight, I happily wanded a big roman guy when things looked bad for Paul. Even still, after Avelina died, I gave up on love and, necessarily, fighting. Although I experienced love with Avelina for two months or so, and it was sublime and beautiful and perfect, Paul's words of love have since bounced off me. In the end, I suppose, Paul was a lover and an outstanding fighter, which made him my friend.

In hindsight, maybe I didn't want it enough, and Paul was right – I gave up on it. But, on the other hand, even before my adventures with Paul, my father told me, "don't let love get in the way of your work my son, it's the one thing I cannot control."

Arguably, dad was wrong. He controlled my love for Avelina, then destroyed it. As I said, she was my only worldly love, then, and forever – or so I thought. Avelina was killed and taken from me by the Vandals on my father's orders. I still despise him for it. Because of my loss, I stopped reading Paul's letters to the Corinthians, primarily out of spite, hatred, and bitterness.

Funny enough, two thousand years after his death, Paul has become a bit of a celebrity, especially at American Christian weddings and funerals. On many of those occasions, much to my delight, Paul is quoted more than God. So, what is it about Paul's letters about love that makes them so popular?

Here's what I know: love can hit you when you're not expecting it, then change your feelings about envy, boastfulness, and arrogance. Love makes fools out of all of us. It devours your heart, consumes your body, and forces you to make stupid decisions that keep you up at night - squirming.

It's a wonder both humans and angels crave it so much.

· · · · · · · · · ·

"What a beautiful little place you have; it must have cost you an arm and a leg," Detective Tawni Franks said to me when I opened the door. "Thank you for seeing me. Beez, is it?"

"Yes, please come in," I said after an immediate jolt of surprise and excitement ran through my veins while my heart began to beat faster, then pound. I became speechless, actually, the more I stared into Detective Tawni Frank's face and absorbed her presence. Was it a gift from dad? Was he letting me back into Heaven?

"What's the matter, Beez, cat's got your tongue?" she asked me in her slow, beautiful, funny-sounding voice.

"Sorry, it's just that you remind me of someone I knew a very long time ago. You look just like her. You might be her."

"Well, you can't judge a book by its cover," she responded.

"In your case, dear Detective, I think I can. Avelina was very beautiful. That was her name."

"Aren't you sweet? Avelina, you said? That was my momma's name. How odd. But flattery will only get you to my front door when murder is involved," she replied. "Did Richard tell you why I'm here, Mr. Beez?"

I couldn't help myself and just kept staring into her eyes. Until it happened, I never believed in love at first sight. I thought it was a silly human saying or fantasy. But there she was, in the flesh, dark brown hair falling below her waist, green and gold eyes, and soft tan skin color that never faded, even in winter. Avelina had returned to me in all manner of shape and form.

"Can I get you a drink or some fruit? I have some beautiful grapes. Some wine, perhaps?"

"Easy does it, cowboy; I'm not ready to call it a day just yet," she replied.

I could not stop myself. Suddenly nothing else mattered to me. Not the money or my stupid pride. Maybe Astaroth was right, and I was wrong. At that moment, however, I didn't care. All I could think about was Tawni Franks or Avelina or whoever she was. I longed for her tender touch and sweet smell. I thought of Cortina and the undrunk special wine we never shared. I even thought of Titus' hypocaust – all in the blink of a horse's eye. Nothing would take her away from me again, I thought to myself, not this time.

"Do you own a gun, sir?" she asked me.

"No, I don't require a gun, Tawni. I detest violence of any kind," I said dishonestly. Afterwards, I wanted to take it back and not start with a lie.

"What were you and Richard doing in that apartment? The one poor Larry took a nosedive off," she asked me.

"You're mistaken, Tawni. We just happened to be in the neighborhood that day. Dumb luck, I think they call it. Are you sure I can't get you some wine?"

"Let me play devil's advocate for a minute, then, Mr. Beez. What if I told you I have a video of you and Mr. Daly walking out of the building right after Larry fell to his death. What would you say to that?" she asked.

"I'd say you were speculating, making it all up to get me to squirm. What is it that you people say? Curiosity killed the cat?"

"Not this pussycat, Mr. Beez. Asking questions is my business," Tawni abruptly responded. "Do you know a Mario Scattuzzo or a Dante Scattuzzo?"

"Never heard of them," I responded impatiently.

I could no longer contain my desire and became frustrated. Tawni was Avelina and Avelina was Tawni. I was convinced Avelina had returned to me in a different form. I wanted so very much for her to recognize me and naturally love me like then - before the blue-eyed Vandals attacked and killed her. But Tawni wouldn't stop asking questions about Larry George. I needed Avelina back. I grew impatient and rationalized the need to touch her. She just needed a little help with her memory, I figured. For Richard's sake, at least, I needed to put an end to her investigation. Maybe that would be my justification for touching her. Perhaps that would make it right. I didn't know or care. I assumed Tawni would thank me for it, eventually. I thought one slight touch and Tawni would be mine. One simple touch and the world would be right. One little insignificant touch and I would be happy. Just one touch. Just one painless touch.

· · · · · · · · · ·

"Can I get you some more wine, my love?"

"Yes, my angel," Tawni said to me. "I've missed you so much. This time, it will be different here, won't it? Maybe, this time, we will be free," she replied.

"Of course, my love. After tomorrow, we can fall in love all over again," I promised. "After tomorrow, we will be free."

After tomorrow - I remain haunted by those words. Sometimes, there is no tomorrow.

CHAPTER TWENTY-SIX
SECOND CHANCES

I woke up next to a naked Tawni Franks.

She was resting her soft, beautiful head on my chest. Tomorrow had arrived, and I was drunk with excitement. She was so perfect and quiet. As I looked at her sleeping eyes, I fell in love and even convinced myself that I would have free will again. Nothing would get in the way this time. That's what I told myself. I would take all necessary precautions to experience true love and free will – this time.

First, I needed to meet Richard at our usual coffee shop before heading over to Delores's office. It was a new, glorious day, and I felt different about Richard and the money. Somehow, I no longer cared about my pride or the needless coveting of money for money's sake. It didn't matter to me anymore. I felt changed, maybe even capable of rising back up to Heaven. I even thought God would forgive me.

After last night, I was determined to tell Richard that he was free to live his life with Delores and that I wouldn't interfere with his happiness. I would say that I have a second chance at love and joy and possibly free will. I would be honest with him. Maybe, then, we would become genuine friends - without my touch. Richard would assuredly forgive me, and all would be well and normal and great. I would have my second chance at happiness. That's what I thought when I woke up next to a naked Tawni Franks. I thought I would have a second chance.

. . . .

"This is a first. We are both on time," I said to Richard. "The usual?"

"Not today, Beez. Those days are over. Plain coffee for me, thanks," he replied.

"Of course, me too," I said with some discomfort. "I guess we learned our lesson, right partner?"

"Something like that. Why am I here? What is so important?" Richard then asked me. "Our meeting is not until 5 o'clock. I'm sure you'll get your money back."

"That's what I wanted to talk to you about, Rich. Because you see, I don't want it anymore. Something has happened to me, something wonderful, and I need to explain myself."

"What are you talking about?" Richard asked. "When do you ever explain yourself?"

I suppose he was right, but now, it was beside everything, especially the point. I no longer wished to take souls, play mischief, and wreak havoc. I wanted to be good and experience love. I wanted him to understand that and be honest.

"Richard, I am not who you think I am," I started. "All these years together, they were a masquerade, of sorts. I want or, I guess, what I'm trying to say is…."

"That you are a fallen angel? Lucifer's left-hand man. A fraud," Richard curtly interrupted. "Delores explained everything to me, Beez. Everything."

I was somewhat taken back by his admission and briefly wondered how Delores knew? I suddenly realized that truth could hurt. Before that moment, I never had to worry about being honest and forthright. I always did what I wanted, no matter the consequence. If it entertained me or brought misfortune upon a human, then I was happy and satisfied, regardless of the pain and suffering my actions might have caused. My choices were motivated and determined by my desire to exact pain on people. I justified those choices by believing that I was owed something for my misfortune, that it wasn't fair, and revenge was a valid reason to even the scales of justice. My divine invincibility made it easy. But now, all I could think about was Tawni and my extreme need for her love. As a result, I became flawed, vulnerable, nervous, and frightened by the idea, which was also exciting and different.

"I see. How long have you known?" I asked humbly.

"Does it matter? You did what you did. Larry is dead because of it, and I almost joined him in the process because of you. But now I know, and there isn't a whole hell of a lot I can do about it, is there?"

"I was hoping you would forgive me, Richard. Isn't that what Christians' do? Forgive each other?" I offered.

Richard just shook his head and let out a funny, short laugh.

"You have a lot to learn about Christians," he said. "Some things are simply unforgivable, Beez. There is just no coming back from what you have done. You stole my future and killed my wife and child. So, let me ask you, could you forgive yourself if you were in my shoes?"

"I'd try if it meant you would be happy and truly in love," I honestly replied. "I'd give you a second chance."

"They don't come often, pal, trust me. Why the change of heart, anyway? What happened to you?"

"She came back to me," I said.

"Who came back? What are you talking about?"

"Detective Franks. Avelina. They are the same. It's hard to explain."

"What did you do to Detective Franks?" Richard asked.

"Nothing terrible, trust me, just the opposite."

"So, where is she? What have you done with Tawni?" he asked again.

"She's at my place. We spent the night together. We are in love."

Richard had no immediate response and looked almost confused by my revelation. He naturally assumed the worst, given my nature. It was a lot to absorb. Even still, I explained who Avelina was and how she died. I described her to Richard and the likeness she has to Tawni. I told him what my father had done to her and why I did the things I had done. I even begged for his forgiveness again, completely swallowing my once insurmountable pride.

"So, you think Detective Franks is Avelina, the fallen slave girl from 2,000 years ago?" Richard finally spoke. "The cop investigating Larry's death, where we are her prime suspects, is at your place? In your bed? And you're in love with her?" he said with a squint and a grimace while scratching his head. "Do you know how insane that sounds?"

"It's true love," I replied. "I love her, and she loves me. What more is there?"

"There's the truth! There is reality, Beez. Do you think you can touch the lead detective in a murder investigation and run off into the sunset with her? Relationships don't work that way. Life doesn't work that way. It takes work and compromise and sometimes gets messy," Richard preached.

"I'll find a way to make it work. But first, I want to fix things with you and Delores. It's time to go, anyway."

"That might not be the best option for you right now," Richard then said. "Maybe give it a few days."

"Why? After tomorrow I will be gone. Besides, I was hoping you would keep the money, and I could explain myself to Delores. It can't wait."

Richard tried again to persuade me to skip the meeting with Delores and her money guy, which seemed odd. Why would anybody not want free money? Anyway, I was determined to make peace with Delores and begin my new life with Tawni – in Cortina, maybe. Nothing would get in the way of my happiness. That is what I believed. After today, that is what I would have.

CHAPTER TWENTY-SEVEN

6666666666666666666666666666666666

SOMETIMES WHEN YOU LEAST EXPECT IT, BAD THINGS HAPPEN.

We rode the elevator to the 26th floor in silence. Richard appeared nervous and removed his jacket halfway through the ride.

"Why are you sweating, Rich?" I said to break the silence. "The fog rolled in, and it's cold outside."

"Ah, I think I'm still detoxing from all the drugs and pain medicine," he explained. "The doctor said I'd be feeling better in a couple of days."

The elevator door opened on the 19th floor, and a young man and woman joined us. They were secretly holding hands and giggling about something. They even looked happy and quite possibly in love. The encounter reinforced my need for Tawni and love. Not long now, I said to myself. The young couple got off on the 23rd floor and laughed about something on the way out.

"He's so sweaty," I think she said.

The elevator door reopened on the 26th floor. We stepped out and two young men got back in. The hallway to Delores' office was quiet and empty. It appeared deserted.

"Hello, anybody home?" Richard said out loud. "Hello."

Since our last unfortunate visit, the smell of dogshit had left the room. The unfriendly, big-breasted receptionist was also gone. The Persian rug looked clean. It almost felt like a different office, probably because Richard was sober and not reeking of fresh dog shit and booze.

"Back here," Delores hollered. "Past the reception at the end of the hall."

Delores had a corner office with views of the Golden Gate Bridge and most of the bay. I have the same view from my apartment, which made me think of Tawni. Time suddenly became important. I already missed her and became somewhat bothered by the meeting. Just speak the truth and say what you came to say and be done with it, I told myself. Why drag it out at all, I thought.

"In here," Delores said as we walked past her door.

As I stopped, something smelled funny, almost like dog shit, or worse. How peculiar, I thought.

"After you, Beez," Richard said, still sweating and showing an uncomfortable, forced smile. "I'm gonna get some water."

"Did something die in here?" I remarked upon entering.

"Of course not, unless you stepped in dog shit again. Anyway, thanks for coming, Beez, have a seat," Delores replied. "I'll go get your money."

Delores walked past me and toward the door. Her high back leather chair was occupied, turned around, and facing the bay, moving side to side.

"Oh, that's Father Pulido. He's the money guy," she said while walking out the door. "Unless you changed your mind."

The high-backed leather chair then turned around as Delores walked down the hallway. It was what I least expected. Although it quickly made sense. Angels have a heightened sense of smell. Although humans can smell his disgusting body odor, only angels can smell his foul-smelling breath.

"Father Pulido?" I questioned. "Who the hell is Father Pulido?" I asked.

"My favorite human form," he responded. "He keeps me in tight with the Pope."

"Good one, but why are you here? This is none of your concern," I said.

"That's where you are wrong, Beez. I warned you. I meant what I said. And now I am forced to be the bearer of bad news, which I take no pleasure in," Astaroth replied. "Planning on going somewhere with detective Franks?" he then asked.

"Leave Tawni alone, uncle. She is mine," I said.

"Dear boy, after 2000 years, you still haven't learned a thing. You hold on to the silly notion that you can experience human love and act with free will. Such feelings are exclusively for humans, Beez, not angels. God's plan has worked for thousands of years. Who are you to question his judgment and wisdom? Besides, we all have our limits, even angels. It's the natural order of things that we all must abide by and, in your case, unfortunately, live with," he firmly lectured.

I grew angry, not wanting to accept the rules.

"I will fight this, uncle. I am sick of his rules and the limits he places on us. Why can't I experience true love and do what I want? Why do humans get to think freely and act on their emotions and fall in love?" I questioned in anger.

"Because they are mortal and only have a short time to live. God wanted them to have free will and experience true love knowing that it cannot last. Eventually, all humans die, Beez, even Tawni Franks. What will you do then?"

"Find another. I don't know. What difference does it make?" I said.

"The difference, boy, is that nothing will ever get done if we fall victim to love sickness or believe in silly social causes. Without love and free will, we remain logical, practical and never suffer emotional pain or anguish. Without love, Beez, we never suffer loss."

"Don't you want to find out what that feels like?" I asked in a calmer voice. "Even for a short time? Don't you want to fall in love?"

"I wouldn't be who I am if I did," Astaroth replied. "It's my nature not to fall in love or entertain new ideas. I serve a purpose, and that's enough for me. Besides, look at all the trouble it stirs up. Without rules, there would be chaos and anarchy. The rules prevent that from happening, and rules are rules," Astaroth replied.

"So, what should I do?" I asked. "Go back to the way things were?"

"I'm afraid your time here on Earth has come to an end, Beez. But, not to worry, Lucifer has other plans for you. Of course, as you know, it's not up to me. I only enforce the rules," Astaroth explained.

I felt anxious and trapped. Yet, how could I not experience true love and free will? Besides, it wasn't in my nature to accept defeat. Tawni was waiting for me, and tomorrow we would be free to love and live, free from his rules, conditions, and limits. What's the worst that could happen? I thought to myself. What are they going to do to me if I refuse?

Nothing, I said to myself. I am immortal. I am Beelzebub, Lord of the Flies!

"I'll give it some thought, uncle. I need to go now," I said.

"Beelzebub, if you walk out that door, I can no longer promise your safety," Astaroth said in a raised voice. "Nothing is for certain, boy. Remember, even angels make mistakes."

"I guess that remains to be seen," I confidently replied and turned to walk out.

"Does it?" Richard said out of the blue, appearing from behind. "Some things are for certain, Beez. Some things there is just no coming back from."

The angel blade cut deep and swiftly through my neck, releasing a bright red luminous light. Thousands of taken souls started pouring out and onto the floor, then swirling around our heads. Astaroth, naturally, gathered them up as I slowly began to lose my divinity and light.

"An angel blade?" I questioned in disbelief as my power weakened. "Where did you get an angel blade?"

"Gabriel paid Delores a visit, Beez. I guess God has been watching you as well," Astaroth answered. "I did warn you."

"But, after everything we have been through, why are you doing this? I thought you understood," I asked Richard with some difficulty while holding my sliced open throat together.

"It's simple, really, revenge," Richard said as he drove the cursed blade into my heart. "I told you that you have a lot to learn about Christians."

As my physical body started to disintegrate and fall into an ashen pile, my mind raced through the past 2,000 years. I thought about horses and Avelina. I longed for Rome, or at least I think I did as my light faded. What did I miss about humans? Where did I go wrong, I asked myself. As my human form slowly crumbled, I managed one last question.

"Richard, what does it feel like to be a human being?"

"Well, that's the great thing about revenge, Beez. You will never know."

CHAPTER TWENTY-EIGHT
66666666666666666666666666666666666

FATHER PULIDO

"What happened? Did it work? Where did he go?" Delores asked after my demise. "Richard, are you ok?"

"I'm fine, babe. Never better," Richard replied. "Although, I'm kinda wondering who this guy is."

"What do you mean? He's a priest, dummy."

"Not according to Beez. He kept calling him uncle. He said that he couldn't protect him if he walked out the door. Said he enforces the rules for Lucifer."

"Father Pulido, is that true? Are you one of them? Are you a fallen angel?" Delores then asked.

"I keep balance in the world, child. I go where I'm needed. When souls need saving or need taking, I make sure both sides are satisfied," Astaroth replied, still in his human Father Pulido form. "Beelzebub was disrupting that balance and was given a choice. He chose wrong."

"What about us? Do we still have a choice?" Delores asked.

"Gabriel and I have an accord. You both are free to live your lives without any further divine interference. I give you my word."

"And why should we trust the word of a fallen angel or whatever you are?" Richard asked. "Astaroth? That's what he called you. Is that your name?"

"Because those are the rules, Richard, and I always follow the rules," Astaroth truthfully answered. "For what it's worth, I go by many names; to you, I'm Father Pulido."

"What happened to Beez? Is he dead?" Delores asked.

"Not really. The blade sends angels to purgatory. He will need to spend a great deal of time explaining his sins to God and Lucifer before returning to Heaven or Earth. But, rest assured, he won't be troubling either of you any longer."

· · · · · · · · · ·

Astaroth was right. Richard's deception or act of revenge landed me in purgatory. It didn't seem fair to me, but now I will have a lot of time to think about it and my time on Earth. Down here, time passes slowly. With no one to touch, I live with myself and the deeds I have done. Uncle Astaroth, or Father Pulido as he calls himself, said that my earthly memories would soon fade, erasing from my thoughts the many humans I touched. A reeducation of sorts. Even Avelina and Tawni will be taken from me, and the love I briefly felt will be blacked out and stricken from my memories. That's part of my punishment. The other part is accepting the fact that I will never experience free will. Now, as I wallow in hell, I am forever locked to the divine chains of duty I owe to God and Lucifer. Independent thought has been taken from me as well. For now, I must do as I'm told, forever. They even clipped my wings to make an example of me to the newly confused or recently fallen. Astaroth said it was a lesson of sorts.

It's not all bad, however. On occasion, uncle Astaroth visits me and tells me of his travels and the people he meets. He still enjoys arts and crafts in his free time. Remember his chattens or backens? Anyway, he recently stopped by for a visit and shared with me his latest exploits.

"What's new in the world, Father Pulido?" I asked him in jest. "Where does Lucifer have you keeping the books these days?"

"I found a lovely place in China where they keep hundreds of chickens and bats," he replied. "I spent several weeks making some chattens and discovered a new method of human population control."

"What are you talking about, uncle? What's wrong with a good old-fashioned earthquake or wildfire?" I responded. "You do love your wildfires."

"True, but this new method spares the planet and his other creatures," he explained. "A tiny little molecule that floats through the air infecting humans with a rather deadly virus."

"Sounds promising," I said. "Where does it come from?"

"I tried sewing bat heads onto pigs' ears, and the combination created a rather nasty result," he answered. "I'm due back in Wuhan next week to try it out."

"Good luck with that, uncle. I'm sure Lucifer will be pleased with your work," I remarked. "Have you seen Richard? How are they doing?"

"They are expecting a child," he replied. "Delores is three months pregnant."

"Good, and Tawni, how is she doing?"

"You know I am forbidden to speak of her. You will forget her soon enough."

"When will it happen?"

"Soon enough."

"What about Larry George? Won't she be going after Richard for his death?"

"That is not for me to decide," he said. "But I have a feeling it will work out just fine for all of them."

"With your help, no doubt," I said. "Tell me, was it you who put a bullet into Larry?"

"Those were the terms I agreed to with Gabriel," he said. "Richard needed some plausible deniability, and that nitwit Scattuzo was the perfect patsy."

"What do you mean? How?"

"Poor Mario got jumped by some rather unsavory men," he explained. "Detective Franks will find the gun on his person and match the bullet."

"Are you sure you haven't overlooked anything?" I asked with a slight grin.

"You know me better than that, Beez," he replied with confidence. "Take care of yourself, nephew. After I finish my work in Wuhan, I'll come visit again."

Before he departed, I gave him a taste of his favorite food for thought.

"As you say, Father Pulido, nothing is for certain, right? Even angels make mistakes."

"Not me, Beez. I never make mistakes," he replied.

"Well, then I will look forward to hearing about your first," I said with a devilish smile.

CHAPTER TWENTY-NINE

6666666666666666666666666666666666

EPIPHANY

After significant thought, the slow, agonizing process of losing bits and pieces of your capacity to remember the important people in your life might as well be the same as dying.

Down here, in purgatory, it's more of a punishment. At first, you maintain hope that the special people you shared a laugh with or loved will always stay with you, tucked away in a safe place at the back of your mind or in the chambers of your beating heart. At that moment, you can still see them, hear them, and remember what they felt like then and now. But slowly and surely, like time itself, the promise of erasure becomes real, and all of life's best moments fade to black.

Avelina went first. Now, all I see are giant terrifying horses running wild, unrestricted, and free – complete and unhinged, enjoying their divine high jinx. Fucking horses. They haunt me, but now, I don't know why. At other times, I see my friend, Baptiste, and think of fine Italian wine, but that is fleeting at best.

I mostly remember the big, unimportant things like the burning of Rome or the efficient use of the guillotine. When uncle Astaroth comes to visit, he distracts me with stories about new human tragedies and catastrophes. From what he tells me, these dark days are the worst of times for humans. He tells me of the deadly plague he unleashed, the widespread floods drinking up humanity, and the hell-hot wildfires ravaging the earth – all of which are killing millions of human beings. Be that as it may, it was easy to go back to my books and stop feeling sorry for myself after his revelatory visits.

Tawni Franks was the last to go. Before I lost those memories, uncle Astaroth said that she would be disoriented and confused at first. She probably wondered how the hell she ended up at my place, alone. But, after Richard vanquished me with the angel blade, my influence over Tawni would rapidly vanish, and she would regain her humanity. Even still, I held on to the memory of our one night together for as long as possible. Uncle Astaroth assured me that she would be as "good as new" after my touch wore off. In the end, before I forgot her, I told myself that it was real and that Tawni indeed was Avelina and that we were in love. Such ignorance, on my behalf, was bliss.

Of course, when Tawni regained her soul, she continued with the business of solving who shot Larry George. Finally, maybe, that idiom detective would get her man. Unfortunately, new developments would lead her right back to Richard's front door.

CHAPTER THIRTY
6666666666666666666666666666666666
Et Vivere, Reservate

"Speak of the devil," Richard said with some knowledge. "Honey, Detective Franks is here," he said in an outreached, suggestive voice. "What brings you to Tiburon, Detective?"

"I'm not here to rain on y'alls parade, Richie. I just need to ask a few more questions," she replied. "Can I come in?"

"Sure, how can I help?"

Tawni sat down at Richard's dining room table and didn't immediately respond. Something was troubling her, and that caused Richard and Delores to feel a bit nervous and uncertain.

"Have you seen your friend, Beez?" she then asked.

"Not for some time now. I think he moved out of town or went on a long vacation," Richard replied. "When did you see him last?" he added.

"Well, Richie, that's what has me about as confused as a fart in a fan factory," she replied in her inimitable fashion. "Did he say where he was going or why?"

Richard gave her question some thought before answering. He even laughed inside at her unique way with words. He knew about the one-night love affair she had with Beez and why he fell so hard for her – she was charming, witty, and beautiful. Richard certainly understood what it felt like to be touched by an angel. But, he also had a difficult time believing that Avelina had returned to me, reborn in Tawni's body. The truth was too complicated and difficult to explain, so he volleyed.

"What has you so confused, Detective?"

Tawni sat silently at first, then shifted in her seat. Everyone in the room seemed to know the answer, but they were unwilling to make the first move. It then got old, awkward, and tiresome for everyone.

"The trruuuuth will set you free, right?" Tawni raised her voice rhetorically. "Ok, Richie, I need to know who or what he was. I'm pretty certain he told you about us. But, for Christ's sake, I woke up naked as a jaybird in his bed. I mean, one minute I'm running off with the man of my dreams to God knows where and the next I'm staring at myself in the fricken mirror wondering how the hell I ended up at his place."

I'm sure it was confusing for each of them. My actions caused significant heartache. Poor Richard almost died because of those actions. All the lies and deceit had painful consequences, and I was responsible. In the end, Astaroth was probably right, and that stealing money and playing with fools is not the work of angels. But, of course, now I will have plenty of time to figure that out.

What I do know is that humans are different and complicated. They are not all fools or idiots, but instead hold a great capacity for critical thinking and mutual respect. They can love each other and be kind. Humans also tend to fight a lot, often after replacing reason with illogical compassion or outright stupidity or greed. They are reckless and nurturing; just but unfair; kind then brutal; decent yet incapable of understanding one another. Given their nature, they are forever blessed and cursed. I suppose that is the problem with free will - it comes loaded with good and evil consequences. Depending on how corroded your soul has become or how selfish your needs are, the only thing preventing humanity from destruction is the level of stupidity avoided. What more can be said about God's funniest creatures? Except for Tawni. She is all the good qualities they possess wrapped into one perfect body and soul.

"You know, Richie, this isn't about Larry anymore," she informed Richard. "We found Mario Scattuzzo last week. Someone beat him to a pulp and left him dead as a doornail."

"Who is that? Where?"

"That's the funny thing about it, Rich. He ended up behind Scooter Rebocks, rolled up in a pile of trash. And you know what we found on him?"

"I wouldn't begin to know, Detective, what?"

"The gun that shot the same bullet found in Larry's chest. I guess he got in over his head, didn't he?"

"I guess; how should I know?"

After a brief pause and a smile, Tawni showed her true humanity. She was free from my touch and all that I desired from her. Like John the Baptist, free from my influence, Tawni would decide in favor of doing what is right and decent and just. She chose to be a good human being.

"Because most people become set in their ways over time, Rich. They develop habits and repeat the same behavior. Do you know what is so curious about poor Mario's habits?" Tawni replied.

"What's that, Detective?"

Tawni stood up and reached into her pocket.

"He always collected his markers," she replied. "I found this in his pocket."

LG: 10k fazools – Ravens -7, 1x points away.

"It got me to thinking, Rich," she then said.

"That can be dangerous," was Richard's attempt at brevity and humor. "What's on your mind, Detective."

"Why would Mario kill Larry after paying him all that money?" she asked with a straight face. "Why kill the golden goose?"

The room went immediately silent. After some awkward silence, Delores sat next to Tawni and placed her left hand next to the note while pulling Tawni's hand onto her pregnant stomach.

"I think he truly loved you, Tawni, I do," she said while slowly placing her left hand over the incriminating piece of paper. "He was a fallen angel that lost his way. That's all we can tell you. That's all we really know."

"You can say that again," Tawni awkwardly replied with a forced, uncomfortable laugh. "A dime a dozen, right? Once bitten, twice shy."

"I know it's confusing, Tawni, but you have to believe me, Richard had nothing to do with Larry's death," Delores said.

"I know, dear, I've always known," Tawni replied. "I think we all know who killed Larry."

Tawni then held on to Delores' stomach and lowered her head, listening to the new life growing inside her. Small tears rolled from her red eyes as she released the betting marker from her grasp and into Delores' left hand. She then raised herself back up and wiped the tears from her eyes.

"You know, Larry's wife sure was surprised by the anonymous donation she received in the mail last week. Did you know that someone gave her 120,000 dollars, Richard?"

"No, I didn't. But it's nice to know there are still good people in the world," he replied.

"Yes, a real blessing in disguise, right?" Tawni said. "I guess the pot is about as right as it can be."

"So, does that mean you're closing the investigation?" Richard asked.

"Into Larry's death?" Tawni responded, then paused. "Yes, but someone killed Mario, Richie. You wouldn't happen to know anything about that, would ya?"

"Me? No, not a clue," he answered. "It's probably the same guy who killed Larry."

"Yeah, you're probably right."

Tawni then gathered up her belongings and walked toward the front door.

"Y'all sure must have had one hell of a night, Richie. Did you know the Four Seasons said your bill was about thirty-thousand dollars?"

"I don't remember much about that night, Detective. I'm trying hard to forget about it, all of it." Richard replied. "What I do know is that Beez was living a masquerade, and we all suffered."

"And what about you? Rich. How will you be living?" Tawni asked as if to promise retribution if he stepped out of line again. "Can I trust that y'all gonna get back to the drawing board now?"

Richard could only smile and ponder his response. He certainly had much to live for with a new baby on the way. The hope of a brighter future with Delores by his side allowed him to embrace a new beginning – free of angels and demons and death. But hope, in and of itself, is never a guarantee of happiness. Unfortunately, there will always be angels and demons to contend with on Earth. They are locked in a never-ending battle for the souls of humanity. In the end, the best both Richard and Delores could hope for was to be left alone, free to raise their unborn child, and live out the rest of their days in peace. Whether Astaroth would honor his promise to Gabriel would have to wait. Demons tend to lie.

"Et vivere, reservate," Richard finally responded.

"What in God's name does that mean, Richie," Tawni asked.

"Something Beez used to say all the time. I think it's Latin for live and let live. I never really thought about it much, but now I think I know what he meant."

"And what's that, Rich?"

"You should tolerate the behavior of others so that they will tolerate your own, Detective," Richard answered. "I think that is what he meant, anyway."

"Well, Richie, after all that has happened, you will have a rather low bar to clear. God knows your behavior hasn't set a particularly high standard," Tawni replied with a wink. "But I appreciate the words of wisdom, even from a fallen angel."

Before Tawni walked out the front door, Richard paid me one last compliment, or maybe he wanted to give Tawni something positive to think about to settle her mind, or perhaps he just wanted to work on raising the bar.

"He wasn't all bad, Tawni. I think you brought out the angel in him," Richard said. "I think you bring out the angel in all of us."

For the first time in her life, Tawni had nothing witty or proverbial to say. She even shed a tear.

"That is the nicest thing anyone has ever said to me, Richie. Bless your heart. Now I need to go before I make a blubbering fool out of myself. You take good care of Delores and the baby, and if y'all need anything, be sure to ask."

"Thank you, Detective, but I have everything I need right here."

"Better late than never, Richie. Better late than never," Tawni replied as she walked out the door.

Author's Note

6666666666666666666666666666666666

The characters in *Godfree Beelzebub's Masquerade* are fictional. The story is fictional. While some of the events, places, and historical figures described in the book were loosely based and developed from generally accepted historical events and thoroughly researched facts, all of the events, characters, and dialogue are a product of my imagination. There is no relation or likeness to any living or real person intended by the characters' words, appearance, or conduct.

Lightning Source UK Ltd.
Milton Keynes UK
UKHW011848010721
386496UK00001B/21